POSEIDON'S ATLANTIS ADVENTURE

THE HUMAN HYBRID EXPERIMENT

GRACE BLAIR

Distribution by Bublish

ISBN: 978-0-9988308-4-1 (paperback)
ISBN: 978-0-9988308-2-7 (eBook)

Names:	Blair, Grace (Grace A.), author.
Title:	Poseidon's Atlantis adventure : the human hybrid experiment / Grace Blair.
Description:	[Lubbock, Texas] : [Modern Mystic Media], [2024] | Series: Atlantis adventure book series ; 1. | Lexile code: 850L. | Audience: Young adult.
Identifiers:	ISBN: 978-0-9988308-3-4 (paperback) | 978-0-9988308-2-7 (eBook)
Subjects:	LCSH: Poseidon (Greek deity)--Fiction. | Mythology, Greek--Fiction. | Time travel--Fiction. | Gods, Greek--Fiction. | Sibling rivalry--Fiction. | Ethical problems--Fiction. | Genetic engineering--Fiction. | Hybridization--Fiction. | Spiritual biography--Fiction. | Quests (Expeditions)--Fiction. | Gifts, Spiritual--Fiction. | Mysticism--Fiction. | LCGFT: Fantasy fiction. | Mythological fiction. | Science fiction. | Action and adventure fiction. | BISAC: YOUNG ADULT FICTION / Fantasy / Historical. | YOUNG ADULT FICTION / Legends, Myths, Fables / Greek & Roman. | YOUNG ADULT FICTION / Science Fiction / Time Travel. | HISTORY / Ancient / Greece. | FICTION / Fairy Tales, Folk Tales, Legends & Mythology. | FICTION / Fantasy / Action & Adventure. | FICTION / Fantasy / Historical. | FICTION / Historical / Ancient. | FICTION / Science Fiction / Time Travel. | FICTION / Thrillers / Historical. | FICTION / Visionary & Metaphysical.
Classification:	LCC: PS3602.L3346 P67 2024 | DDC: 813/.6--dc23

Dedicated to my husband and writing mentor,
John Blair,
whose inspiration and unwavering support
sustained me through the grueling trials
of the writing process.

Asclepeion of Atlantis
Temple of Atlas
Pleiad Strait
Temple of Artemis
Artemis Peninsula
Coves of Artemis
THE LOST CITY
ATLANT

Temple of the Pleiads
Atlantis Bay
Wildwoods Peninsula
The Northern Villages
Northern Watch
Walk of Artemis
Westwards Watch
Western Boundary
Oceanis Orchards
Merope Village
Holy Grove
Poseidon's Pass
North Pass
Asterope's Garden
Electra Fields
Pleione Farmlands
Temple of Poseidon
Alcyone Stables
South Pass
Eastwards Watch
Celaeno Village
Southern Watch
ATLANTIS
Pleione's Pass

PART ONE

OLYMPIANS VS. TITANS

CHAPTER ONE
20,000 B.C.

THE ECHOES OF A CHILLING SILENCE FILLED THE AIR, BROKEN only by the creaking groan of the bronze tombs as they opened. Poseidon's eyes fluttered open, his imposing stature shivering from the cold that clung to his skin like a second layer. His first breath was sharp and icy, piercing his lungs as if it were his very first taste of life. He was not alone; Hades, Hestia, Demeter, and Hera—all gods and goddesses in their own right—emerged from their own tombs.

"What … what has happened to us?" Poseidon gasped, his voice hoarse and unfamiliar to his ears. The uncertainty in this dark, forsaken place gnawed at him. He blinked hard and fought back the threat of danger.

Hades, gaunt and pallid, his black eyes glinting with an unnerving intensity, surveyed their surroundings. His voice was low and somber when he finally spoke. "Tartarus. It seems we have been imprisoned in the depths of the Underworld."

The stench of sulfur assaulted Poseidon's nostrils as he passed through the obsidian walls of Tartarus, a realm of eternal torment. Rivers of fire carved twisting channels through the bleak landscape, casting an infernal glow over the jagged rocks. Wails of anguish echoed from the darkness, the grim chorus accompanying Poseidon on his descent.

Wickedness enveloped them, creeping into every crevice, swallowing all warmth and hope. The air was suffocating and smelled of brimstone and decay. Dampness clung to the walls, leaving streaks of moisture that glistened like the tears of forgotten souls. In the depths of Tartarus, time had abandoned them.

Poseidon took a tentative step forward, his fists clenched, his knuckles white. The stone beneath his feet was cold, its rough texture providing little comfort to his battered body. Determination, his muscles tightening, driving him to explore this place of torment despite his trepidation. He refused to let the unknown shackle him and his kin.

"Stay close," he told the others. "We need to escape this hellish confinement."

As they ventured deeper into Tartarus, their footsteps echoed. Poseidon's calm exterior belied his turmoil within. The weight of uncertainty clung to him like shackles, yet he bore it with the stoicism of one who had faced countless storms. Thoughts swirled like a maelstrom. He would face whatever awaited them, for his loyalty to his family was unbreakable.

"Come on," Poseidon said, his voice shaking with cold and uncertainty. "We need to move."

He strained to penetrate the inky darkness, searching for any sign of hope. Every shadow seemed to morph into a monstrous figure, ready to pounce. In this realm of torment, he found no solace, only an ever-deepening abyss.

Hera, her regal demeanor momentarily faltering, cast a glance back at the obsidian walls they had passed through, her brow furrowed in contemplation. "This is no ordinary prison," she mused, her voice carrying a hint of uncertainty.

Hades, who walked behind Poseidon with a grim determination, turned to face her. His eyes held a rare glimmer of empathy, softening their usual intensity. "No, it is not," he admitted. "Someone, or something, has orchestrated this."

The thought that there might be a force capable of imprisoning them within Tartarus itself sent a sensation that mingled with the icy grip of the Underworld.

Hestia's eyes brightened, her gaze shifting to the rivers ablaze with intensity, etching their path through the terrain.

Hades spoke with a quiet intensity, his voice carrying a newfound sense of purpose. "If we can manipulate the elements here, we might just shape our own destiny."

Demeter shook her head. "No, I don't think so. The massive river of bubbling, hot brimstone goes forever."

Discouraged by this revelation, Poseidon pressed forward. His steps were now slowed by reality. The darkness still clawed at him. His determination burned brighter, a beacon in the abyss.

With every step they took, they forged a path through the torment, defying the odds and unraveling the mysteries of their prison. Their powers intertwined and their bonds grew stronger, inching them closer to a hidden truth that would reshape their understanding of the world.

"Keep moving," he urged his siblings, his voice strained but resolute. "This place will not break us." The echoes of their footsteps now resonated not only with despair, but also with the promise of liberation. In the heart of Tartarus, where despair and hope intertwined, the gods of Olympus embarked on a journey that would challenge their very essence and force them to confront the shadows that lurked within their own hearts.

In the depths of Tartarus, Poseidon led the way, naked and shivering, his mind a whirlwind of fear and uncertainty. But with every step, his resolve grew stronger, an unbreakable tether binding him to his family and their shared fate.

"Forward," he repeated as they plunged deeper into the darkness, the unknown stretching out before them like an insatiable void.

"Watch your step," he warned as they navigated a treacherous stretch of rocky ground. "We don't know what lies beneath the surface."

"Or above it," Hestia whispered, her gaze fixed on the shadows that seemed to dance and shift around them. The air crackled with tension as they pressed onward, Poseidon leading them deeper into the realm of torment and despair.

"By the gods, what is this place?" Demeter murmured, her voice barely audible.

"An abomination," Poseidon answered, the words like a curse on his lips. "But we will escape its clutches. We must." His voice rising above the oppressive silence, he continued, "Courage, my siblings. We are the gods of Olympus, and mere shadows and darkness will not defeat us." His bold words seemed to galvanize his siblings, their steps growing surer as they followed him through Tartarus.

The air in Tartarus hung heavy with the smell of dead bodies decaying. Each breath of sulfur and brimstone Poseidon took burned his lungs like a thousand fiery daggers. The sound of dripping water echoed through the cavernous expanse, punctuating the suffocating silence that enveloped them.

Poseidon tried to ignore the shivers that racked his body. He scanned the shadows, searching for any signs of escape or hope.

He could feel the dampness seeping into his bones, but he fought back the urge to collapse from exhaustion, knowing that giving in would mean certain death for him and his siblings.

"Strange," he murmured, more to himself than to anyone else. "These walls ... they seem to be alive."

Indeed, the walls seemed to pulse beneath his fingers, their cold and slimy surfaces whispering ancient secrets as they writhed and contorted. The sensation both fascinated and repulsed Poseidon, but he couldn't afford to dwell on it for long. They had to break free from this confinement.

"Stick together," he commanded, his voice a low growl. "And keep your wits about you. Tartarus is an ever-changing labyrinth, and we must be resourceful if we are to survive its treachery."

Poseidon's instincts guided him through the oppressive darkness. Now and then, he listened intently for any clues that might help them find their way—the faintest rustle of movement, the distant echo of tortured souls, the subtle vibrations of the ground beneath their feet.

"Something isn't right," Hestia whispered over the relentless *drip-drip-drip* of water. "I can feel a presence ... ancient and powerful."

"Whatever it is, we must be prepared to face it," Poseidon replied, his tone grim but resolute. "We are not alone in this place, and our journey through Tartarus will be fraught with peril."

But even as he spoke these words, a deep sense of curiosity stirred within him, an insatiable desire to uncover the mysteries that lay hidden within the depths of Tartarus. He knew they were walking a dangerous path, but the unknown beckoned him like a siren's call, offering secrets and knowledge that he could scarcely imagine.

"Stay vigilant," he told himself, shaking off the allure of the darkness. "This is no place for idle curiosity."

They reached a source of light—a cluster of luminescent fungi clinging stubbornly to the damp stone walls. Poseidon knelt, examining the strange growths with great interest. "Curious," he mused, his fingertips brushing against the cool, slimy surface of the fungi. This is a completely new life form for me.

"Let us continue," he urged, rising to his feet and leading the way once more. Their journey took them through a labyrinth of twisting passageways and cavernous chambers, each one more foreboding than the last. Despite the ever-present darkness and the oppressive atmosphere, Poseidon's determination never wavered.

"Forward," he commanded, his voice resonating with the authority of the seas themselves. "Together, we shall rise from the depths of Tartarus and return to the world above."

"Agreed," Hades murmured, his gaze lingering on the shifting shadows as if trying to divine what horrors might lie within.

Poseidon nodded, his heart pounding in his chest like a drumbeat heralding an impending storm. He knew that each step they took deeper into Tartarus brought them closer to potential danger, but he also understood that turning back was not an option. Abandoning their quest was not an option after coming this far.

As they advanced cautiously, the air grew frigid, Poseidon felt a chill. His breath came in white clouds of frosty mist as he fought to suppress the shivers that racked his body. He clenched his fists and steeled himself, refusing to show any sign of discomfort before his brothers.

"Listen!" Hades hissed sharply, his eyes widening with apprehension.

In the silence, Poseidon could barely make out a distant clang, like metal scraping against stone. An invisible hand seemed to seize his heart, its icy grip sending a shudder through him.

They hastened onward, the ominous sound growing louder until it echoed off the walls of a massive chamber. Ancient runes glowed like spiritual fire, reverberating with an eerie energy.

At its center lay three Hecatoncheires—Cottus, Brierius, and Gyges—as well as three cyclopes, Brontes, Steropes, and Arges, who slumbered heavily in the oppressive atmosphere.

Poseidon whispered urgently, "Let's move carefully; we don't want to wake them."

CHAPTER TWO

The siblings huddled into the granite cavern, their bodies trembling from a mixture of fear and cold. Hestia, the eldest at eighteen years, tried her best to comfort her younger siblings as they passed the one-eyed monsters and hundred-hander giants.

As they clung to each other, the air felt heavy with despair. The walls were slick with condensation that matched the cold sweat on their skin. The only light came from a thin crack in the stone ceiling above, casting a dim beam onto the dirt floor. They heard other tormented souls groaning and whispering in the chamber. The scent of mold and decay filled their nostrils, a constant reminder of their dire situation.

The faint sound of footsteps echoed through the cold and damp corridors of Tartarus. With every step, a glimmer of hope surged through the siblings. They saw a tall figure approaching in the dim light.

The figure whispered, "Hush, be quiet. I am here to help."

Poseidon's began to adjust to the darkness. Torches mounted to gigantic stone walls burned.

In the torchlight, the youth smiled, his eyes bright blue. "Don't be afraid," he said reassuringly. "I am your brother, Zeus," he continued, his voice like music from an angel's harp. "Here, drink this." He passed the wineskin to Poseidon, who grabbed it and guzzled.

Distraught, Poseidon asked, "What happened to us?"

Zeus sat down on the granite floor and whispered, "Our father, Cronus, the god of time, imagined his children, his brothers, your uncles, the cyclopes, and the Hecatoncheires would take his power, as he had done to his father, Uranus. So when each was born, he stopped their hearts out of fear and cast everyone down to Tartarus. Our mother, Rhea, tricked our father by replacing me with a stone wrapped in swaddling when I was born. Being the youngest son, she hid me from our father. She took me to a cave at the foot of a holy mountain and cared for me there."

Poseidon, his eyes red-rimmed and sunken, his face the color of chalk, shook his head in disbelief as he breathed in the dark plan. "Why were you saved?"

Zeus reached for the wineskin, black curls of hair falling forward across his forehead. He took a drink and let out an enormous sigh. "When I became a man, she needed me to rescue her children. Mother poured a magic potion into Cronus's wine to break the enchanted sleeping spell. Mother sent me to release you from Father's sorcery. Listen carefully, my siblings. Our father imprisoned us here because he fears our power. He believes that if we were to unite, we would overthrow him and assume control of the world."

Hera's brow furrowed as she processed this revelation. "But why? Why does he fear us so? We are his children, not his enemies."

"I'm aware Tartarus has been your home all your life," Zeus said to Hera. Your bodies have grown and developed while in suspended animation. So have your abilities as gods. Each of you has a special talent. When we leave here, I will help you discover what your inherent gift is."

"The hunger for power has always consumed Father," Zeus explained, his voice tinged with bitterness. "He dethroned his own father, Uranus, to seize control of the cosmos. And now, he fears the same fate awaits him. His own paranoia and ambition blind him."

"Then we must escape," Hestia declared, her resolve growing stronger by the moment. "We cannot remain here and let our father's twisted desires dictate our fates."

Zeus nodded. "Agreed. But we must be cautious. Escaping from Tartarus is no easy feat. Cronus filled the labyrinthine corridors with dangers beyond your wildest imagination, and we must confront Campe, the fearsome guard who watches over this place." His eyes narrowed as he gazed at his siblings, seeing the flicker of fear in their expressions. "Are you prepared for the trials that lie ahead?"

Poseidon's newfound determination led him to say leaving is better. "We will stand together, united against our father, and reclaim our freedom."

"Then let us begin," Zeus said, his words heavy with purpose. "I have memorized the map of Tartarus. We need to make haste and leave this treacherous prison after we are free. Stay close, and trust in one another. Together, we can overcome anything Cronus throws in our path."

Poseidon's gaze flickered with uncertainty as he glanced at his siblings; their faces were etched with the same unspoken fears and questions that weighed heavily on his own mind.

"Zeus." Hades spoke up, his voice reverberating through the cold stone corridor. "What assurance do we have that he won't recapture us after we leave this prison?"

"Believe me, brother," Zeus replied, the confidence in his tone both reassuring and commanding, "I've spent years devising a plan to free us from Cronus's tyranny. We will not only slip past his guards but also unite against him, so he'll never dare hurt any of us again. We cannot live our lives in fear of failure. Our strength lies in our unity, and together, we are unstoppable. Trust in yourself and in our bond as a family."

Poseidon's chest tightened with a mixture of anxiety and a new sense of purpose. He knew that his loyalty to his family was unwavering, but the idea of finding his place among them still haunted him. As they made their way through the winding corridors of their prison, Poseidon's thoughts raced like waves crashing on the shore.

"Watch out!" Hades cried, pulling Poseidon back just as a treacherous spike shot out from the wall.

"Thanks," Poseidon muttered, momentarily shaken from his internal turmoil. He realized he needed to focus on the present, on surviving the dangers that lay ahead, rather than dwelling on what might wait for them outside of Tartarus.

As they rounded a corner, a spine-chilling screech echoed through the dimly lit corridors. The siblings froze in their tracks, every muscle in their bodies tensing.

Poseidon looked back at his siblings. He heard a tiger growl in the distance. "Zeus, what is that noise? Is there any danger around us?"

Zeus turned around to see the guard of Tartarus, Campe, run toward them with twenty ropes of slime dripping off her body. The tentacles on her face writhed and jiggled, and five extra ones moved out from beneath her scales and thrust forward with pinpricks on their ends.

An aura of malevolence radiated from her monstrous form, which was covered in scales that shimmered a sickly green under the flickering torchlight. Her upper body resembled that of a woman. Her red eyes gleamed with hunger, and her mouth gaped to reveal a row of razor-sharp teeth. In her clawed hands, she wielded a pair of curved blades that dripped with venom.

"Finally," Campe hissed, her voice a sinister whisper. "I've been waiting for you, children of Cronus."

Terror gnawed at the edges of their resolve, and the siblings exchanged apprehensive glances. Hades clenched his fists, sweat beading on his brow as he warily eyed Campe's venomous blades. Demeter trembled beside her brothers, her hands glowing with the green energy of her powers, a stark contrast to the fear in her eyes.

"Campe, we don't want to fight you," Zeus said, attempting to reason with the monstrous guard. "Our father has imprisoned us unjustly. We only want our freedom."

"Freedom?" she sneered, her eyes narrowing into dangerous slits. "Silence!" Campe roared, her voice echoing through the cavernous chamber. She whipped the air behind her with her serpent tail. "I am bound by blood and honor to serve Cronus, and I will not allow you to defy him!"

"Is there no way we can convince you to let us pass?" Hera asked, her voice trembling but firm.

"Your words are wasted on me," Campe replied, a wicked grin spreading across her grotesque face.

"Then we have no choice," Zeus said, his voice heavy with resignation. He glanced at his siblings, each one nodding in agreement. "We stand together, as family, against you."

"Very well," Campe hissed, her red eyes gleaming with anticipation. "Let us see what the children of Cronus are truly made of."

The danger awakened Poseidon's fearless rage. He became focused. "Zeus, give me the wineskin. Be brave and hold her off until Hestia, Demeter, Hera, Hades, and I can awaken the uncles and the Hecatoncheires."

Zeus, new to the battlefield, was resolute in his determination to make a stand. Despite playing sword games as a child, he had to discover courage he did not know he possessed. He wanted to run away from this conflict, but he knew he needed to stay and protect his older siblings. He could feel his sword shaking in his hands, yet he stood firm and ready to fight.

A wave of anxiety crashed over the young god as he wiped his damp hands on his tunic. With a determined nod, he grasped the hilt of his bronze sword and drew it from its sheath. He was unsteady on his feet. He shouted, "Come get me!" to the beast and prepared to face the Hydra.

Meanwhile, Poseidon guided Hestia, Demeter, Hera, and Hades back to the sleeping-giant uncles. Each of them was wrapped in the tattered clothes of their shrouds. Their limbs looked strange, like those of an insect, hunched and bent.

He gave Hestia, Demeter, Hera, and Hades a dose of the wineskin. The potion strengthened the pure-blooded Olympians from the spell they had fallen into.

Then Poseidon strode to the sleeping, hulking beasts, three Hecatoncheires—Cottus, Brierius, and Gyges—as well as three cyclopes, Brontes, Steropes, and Arges. They roared awake when he slipped a drop of ambrosia down their throat. They sipped the elixir and waded out of the torrents, leaving streamlets of greenish-black water behind. Flailing their multiple hands in the smokey vapors, they stalked about. The thunder of their beating feet on the stone floor shook the cavern.

Tumbling rivers spilled into the churning maw of a large, sulfuryl black lake. Beneath the earth, even below Hades and surrounded by a wall of bronze, Tartarus was a vast place.

Fully awake, Poseidon motioned to his uncles to listen. Pointing to himself and his siblings. "I understand we don't know one another. You are my father's brothers. We are Cronus's children, imprisoned like you because our father fears our powers. Right now, we beg you to join us. We need to help Zeus kill Campe, the monster guard, so we can escape from this prison. We must hurry."

Ready to battle the monster brothers of the Titans, each cyclops stood twenty feet tall with a single eye set in the middle of their forehead. Arges (Light), Brontes (Thunder), and Steropes (Lightning) were master artisans of supernatural skill, possessing enormous strength. The Hecatoncheires, Cottus, Brierius, and Gyges being hundred-handed, could weld hundreds of stones at one time.

The cavern shook as the giant's enormous feet marched out of their nest. Hestia, Demeter, Hera, and Hades ran with Poseidon to battle the vicious guard in Tartarus.

Campe wanted her prize: Zeus himself. Coming close with one of her twenty arms, she tried to grab him with its pincers. He sprinted away on his long legs toward the cave opening as she scuttled after him on her ten feet, her silver fur rippling across her back.

Campe was ready to tear Zeus apart with her teeth and claws. The beast's heads inside her body howled. She chased Zeus into a corner of the cave, where her fangs dripped with saliva, ready to kill.

Poseidon pointed to the cyclopes. "Hold down her arms while Zeus strikes."

Arges, his one eye blazing with fury, roared, "Okay, we will." The three crept toward Campe with brutish tenacity.

Poseidon motioned to the hundred-hander giants while he tugged on his sword. "Throw rocks and brimstone at her while we hold her still. Zeus will deliver the final blow with his sword."

Fearless in the face of danger, Poseidon advanced toward Campe. They came close to where Zeus hid.

"Nothing you do can stop me!" Campe hissed, her voice a sinister melody that sent shivers down their spines.

The giants began hurling hot brimstones at the she-monster.

Campe, alarmed by the hot stone attack, turned her wicked eyes toward them. Her expression was wild with ferocity as she looked at her six attackers. One of Campe's powerful arms snaked out and grabbed for Brontes but missed him.

Steropes signaled his brothers to grab Campe's snake legs while he wrapped his hand around one of her thin coils. He nodded to his brothers as they pinned Campe down. She caught Steropes off guard by lifting him up into the air with one of her coiling reptile arms.

Poseidon screamed at Zeus, "Take your sword and destroy her!"

Zeus, with one powerful slash, cut off Campe's arm.

In a single motion, Steropes plummeted from the sky, hitting the ground with an earth-shaking impact. He charged toward the beast, roaring, "I shall be the one to end her!"

Fiery brimstones rained down on the creature like burning hail, yet she still resisted. "Is that all you got?" Campe laughed.

Three cyclopes fought her. Steropes held her right arms, Brontes held her left tentacles, and Arges punched her giant head.

Poseidon shouted at Zeus, "Now, drive your sword straight into her heart!"

Zeus obliged, leaping onto the writhing creature's chest. With his gleaming bronze sword at one with his heart, he plunged his blade deep within her core. Campe's body convulsed in pain before it fell still; the demon guard of the Olympians was no more.

Poseidon roared to his siblings and uncles, "We must flee at once to the safety of Olympus! Zeus, take the cyclopes and lead us out; I shall follow with our kin, safeguarding our retreat. The Hecatoncheires will be my shield against danger."

Demeter and Hera quivered as they struggled to their feet but collapsed in a heap. Poseidon summoned the Hecatoncheires. "Help them up and guide us back to Olympus."

Poseidon turned to Arges. "In this battle against our evil father and your brother, we fought well together and have found common ground. Let us, the Olympians, cyclopes, and Hecatoncheires, forge an alliance to defeat Cronus. We are forever in your debt for freeing us from this inferno! Please join us on Mount Olympus!"

CHAPTER THREE

POSEIDON WOKE WITH THE TASTE OF SALT AND BLOOD ON HIS tongue. His heart pounded against his chest, as if trying to break free from its cage. He squinted and rolled out of bed, careful not to wake Pero, his pet hawk. In the empty room, he stood and steadied himself against the cool white walls. The faint smell of coke fire lingered in the air.

Insomnia plagued the god of the sea. A week without sleep had left his eyes bloodshot. He paced the Olympian stronghold's marble floor, where the gods discussed things privately.

Led by his cowardly father, Cronus, the war of the Titans against the Olympians had lasted ten years, ending in a stalemate. The Olympians had to win.

A knock on the oak door broke his reverie. Dressed in a loose white tunic, his black, shoulder-length hair in disarray, Poseidon straightened and strode over to open the door.

His mother, Rhea, stood across the threshold. Dressed in a blue silk, floor-length, and hooded cloak, she put her finger to her lips and pushed him into the room. She whispered, "A conspiracy to assassinate the king is underway. Zeus thinks he can slay his father by himself. I am worried. Please stop him."

Poseidon laughed as he crossed his arms. "Oh, Mother. Save your favorite son? Zeus still thinks he is a hero since rescuing us in Tartarus. My brave brother. Let him try. Why not?"

Poseidon saw his mother overwrought and flustered, Rhea broke eye contact. She tugged on her long red braid, sputtering, angry at this weak gesture. "Please, Poseidon. When Zeus decides, there is little we can do. Help him. I am begging you."

From the open bedroom window, the sound of stomping feet and the melodic ring of voices singing spilled into the room. Poseidon hurried and witnessed three cyclopes and a crowd of his people below.

Wearing a tunic and with one shining eye, Arges requested, "Poseidon, Zeus, Hades: we bear gifts. Come, your uncles are here to honor you."

The three bald, one-eyed, shaggy brothers waited next to an open wooden wagon. The scarlet bed of the carriage featured door handles with golden dolphins. Servants of the Olympians singing praises to the gods followed them. They carried little baskets with pomegranates and oranges in them, and two servants at the front sang while others played lyres.

Blinking at the bright light of the sun, Poseidon gazed up into his Uncle Arges's radiant smile.

Brontes, and Steropes crouched low by an open wooden wagon carrying an altar made of bronze. Olympians singing praises to the gods followed the cyclopes.

Brontes and Arges reached into the wagon, retrieved the altar, and transported it to Zeus's feet.

The altar resembled an ancient, megalithic temple: a thirty-foot statue depicting Greek mythology, Dionysus, on a chariot with panthers, made of bronze and gold and decorated with precious gems.

Arges placed his broad, calloused fist over his heart and smiled at the demigods. "We are grateful to you for saving us from your father's hell. We are giving you weapons to help you win the war against the Titans, and as a sign of respect. Please accept this gift as thanks for your bravery in rescuing us from eternal damnation," he said.

Overwhelmed with wonder, Zeus opened his palms. Steropes laid a magical weapon in his nephew's hands. The thunderbolt was thin, larger than Brontes' forearm, but thicker than his thumb. The surface gleamed and was smooth, as if polished by hand. "This will control storms, thunder, and lightning and help steer the course of the entire universe."

Zeus raised the thunderbolt high. Its energy crackled over his skin and down his spine. The power to shatter mountains, to scorch entire armies to ash. This was no gift; it was dominion itself.

A grim smile pulled at his lips. Now, finally, he could seize his destiny. None would dare stand against the king of the heavens armed with thunder itself.

He met Poseidon's uneasy gaze. "Brother, with this mighty bolt, we shall build a new age—together."

Poseidon hesitated, then nodded.

Zeus turned back to Arges, pride and ambition burning in his eyes. "You have my thanks, old friend," he rumbled. "Soon all shall kneel before the thunder."

Poseidon stepped forward. His eyes fixed on an ornate trident resting atop the altar. They'd forged its prongs of imperial gold that gleamed even in the dim light of the cavern. Intricate engravings of roiling waves and fantastic sea creatures adorned the haft. This was no mere weapon; this was the fury of the ocean, given form.

Reverently, Poseidon lifted the trident from its place of honor. Immediately, he felt its power resonating with his essence like the beating heart of the sea itself.

"With this trident, you shall create new lands and command the oceans and all their secrets," Arges intoned. "No ship shall sail beyond your sight; no beast stirs in the lightless depths but by your leave."

Poseidon tightened his grip, and the trident hummed in response. Vast, untamed power—but also a grave responsibility. He met Zeus's gaze. "The seas are wild and unpredictable," Poseidon said. "But the tide flows both ways. With this gift, I shall help guide our people to a new dawn."

Zeus nodded. "Together, we shall build a world to last ten thousand years."

Poseidon hoped it was so. He turned to regard Hades lingering in the shadows behind Zeus. Despite his unreadable face, Poseidon sensed his brother's unease.

Arges, the man of light, pulled from the wagon a metal bident. He remembered the darkness of Tartarus and its suffering without hope or meaning. It had taken making this weapon for Hades to regain his purpose. "This bident is a two-pronged implement that resembles a pitchfork. It is a potent tool, capable of easily tearing humans in half. Use it wisely."

Hades stepped forward to claim his own gift—the cruel, jagged bident that seemed to leach the very light from the air.

Arges promised dominion over death itself. But as Hades lifted the vicious weapon, his black eyes were full of foreboding.

Poseidon prayed the Olympians were not making a terrible mistake.

Zeus clasped Hades on the shoulder, giving him a reassuring smile despite the ominous weapon in his brother's hands.

"Do not look so troubled, brother. This day signifies a new era for all of us. We will bring unprecedented prosperity with these gifts. The thunderbolt, trident, and bident are powerful instruments that our uncles have given us, and we can use them for war. However, it is our responsibility to use them to rule with wisdom and justice."

Hades's expression remained guarded, but he nodded. "Let us hope so."

Arges applauded. "I summon the Olympians to bring your gifts and come forward to the altar."

Arges, Brontes, and Steropes gathered around the rear. Poseidon stood holding his trident, in a breastplate covered with curved fins that shone golden like the sea at sunset. Zeus held his new thunderbolt aloft, its handle crafted from bronze and decorated with detailed carvings of daily life in Olympus. Hades held his bident, its blade double-sided and sharpened on both edges. The handle had leather wrapping and two coins engraved with Cerberus and Hades's helmet.

The cyclopes bowed once more. Poseidon smiled, pride swelling within him. Today marked a momentous change for them all. With tools like the trident, bident, and the thunderbolt, they would be unstoppable. A new era was dawning.

Poseidon's smile faded as he considered the battles ahead. Despite the invaluable gifts from the cyclopes, Poseidon was uncertain about the victory in the battles ahead. The Titans would not go quietly. Cronus and his loyal brothers wielded great power. Thunderbolt alone may not defeat them.

Poseidon sighed, his shoulders slumping under an invisible weight. The outcome of this conflict was pivotal. The destiny of mortals globally was at risk, not just their freedom. If the Titans prevailed, darkness would reign. How many innocent lives would perish?

He thought of his mother, Rhea. She had risked so much, hiding Zeus to save him and, eventually, his siblings from Cronus. Her act of deception had been their only chance of life. Poseidon owed it to her to fight with everything he had.

Looking up, he met Zeus's eyes. Though unspoken, he knew they shared the same doubts and fears. But also, the same sense of purpose. Mortals deserved to be free from the Titans' cruelty.

Poseidon gripped his trident tighter, steeling himself. The path ahead would be arduous. But united with his siblings, he would give his all to end the Titans' rule. Failure was not an option.

With new resolve, Poseidon turned toward the horizon. The moment had arrived to unleash the sea's full power on their foes. A fierce storm was gathering, and he would steer it directly into the heart of the Titans' domain.

CHAPTER FOUR

The grand hall of Cronus's palace glowed with the light of a thousand torches. Servants scurried back and forth, bearing platters laden with rich meats, sweet fruits, and heady wines.

The gods conversed among themselves in joyous tones, like the rushing waters during springtime. Rhea, wife of Cronus, Titan goddess of fertility and motherhood, stood whispering to Theia, the Titaness of Sight and the mother of Helios, Selene, and Eos.

A chorus of strings and singers who stood for the nine Muses entertained the gods with their divine talents. It was a beautiful symphony that played in perfect harmony. The drums hit fast and heavy, reflecting the beat of a heart. The flutes played beautiful trills, like a bird's song.

Hyperion, Titan of Light and father of Helios, the sun, sat chatting with his daughter Selene, goddess of the moon. They dressed all in luxurious fabric and adorned with jewels. Nymphs and servants addressed them. They draped themselves over long sofas and ate delicacies made from the finest ingredients. The gods feasted with music and dance, their movements fluid and graceful.

Then the Titan of Time, Cronus, appeared at the top of the piano Nobile, observing the party and his loyal followers. His magnetic eyes touched every soul in the room before he swept down the monumental staircase. The marble staircase had two rows of columns, where it opened to the vast central court of the palace in Crete. His sudden arrival brought about an intangible excitement in the room. He entered with a majestic bearing, his footsteps reverberating like thundering hooves. His intimidating presence was impossible to ignore.

The gods and goddesses grew silent and drew closer to him without knowing why. He examined each of them, as if he could read all their souls.

The titan of time held a scythe and his harpe in his left hand, symbolizing his rebellion and his ties to fertility and agriculture.

Cronus thought of his father, Uranus, as he clenched the adamantine scythe in his hands. In his mind, he relived the day his mother gifted him with its magical power. The blade shone brightly in the cavern, a lethal glint of mercilessness that vibrated in the very air. Heaving a deep breath and gritting his teeth, he raised the weapon high above his head and brought it down without hesitation. Uranus's anguished cry echoed through the cave as the razor-sharp edge sliced through his flesh and tore away his manhood.

The vibrations from the scythe throbbed through Cronus's muscles as it cut through Uranus's body, cleaving ties between them in a single blow. Justice served without remorse or pity marked the beginning of a new age.

An imposing figure, he commanded attention and bowed his head humbly as the crowd erupted into cheers.

Today, his long silvery hair had wavy curls, while a slick sheen covered his face. Dressed in purple and white finery, he wore a heavy white fur-trimmed cape, black boots, and silver jewelry.

His voice was deep and booming, like thunder on a stormy night. Something else was present underneath it all. His smile beamed across the room. "Welcome to the celebration of the Titans." With a wave of his harpe, he motioned to his guests. "Please gather around the banquet table. Let us enjoy our time together."

Cronus occupied the head of the table. He placed his harpe in a brass holder next to him. He motioned to Agamemnon, the Greek King of Mycenae, to sit next to him on his right.

Agamemnon wore a purple tunic, gold wreath, and sandals; his beard was black. He sat next to Cronus with an imperial smile.

King Tyndareus of Sparta on his left wore a purple and gold tunic. A gold wreath studded with diamonds circled his coiffed, black, shoulder-length hair. His black eyes smiled with recognition of Cronus.

The kings shared an unusual, scornful smile across the table.

A group of royals sat around the king's table chatting and eating. Each is more beautiful than the next.

"My friends," Cronus bellowed, rising to address the room, his voice booming through the dining hall. "Tonight, we celebrate our impending victory against those wretched Olympians!"

A cheer rose from the crowd seated around the table. They raised goblets high, sloshing wine over the rims.

Cronus allowed a thin smile to crack his stony features. He'd waited an eternity for this moment to arrive. His children, the Olympians, planned to overthrow him. "In a time before cities, when humanity was still wild and untamed, I created our Golden Age. I understood no human could take charge without growing proud and unjust."

The mighty Titan pointed to Agamemnon and Tyndareus. "So, I appointed divine kings and rulers with supernatural powers and wisdom to rule over the people of our world. With my vision and their governance, we have flourished for thousands of years in abundance and enjoyed peace, tranquility, and justice." He continued, "If the Olympians win this war, we cannot risk the unrest and hardships that may plague our divine governance."

With a clap of his mighty hands, Cronus summoned the first course. A small army of servants emerged, bearing platters of exotic meats—roast boar with apples, peppered venison, and succulent fowl drizzled in honeyed sauces. As the Titans tore into the feast with greedy fingers, musicians struck up a lively tune on lyres and pipes. Dancers swirled through the hall; their lithe bodies draped in diaphanous silks.

Cronus watched with detached amusement, sipping rich red wine from a goblet. Victory was near. He could feel it. His aspiration was to make the universe tremble once again before him.

The festivities ended with the sound of his scythe hitting the marble ground. All eyes turned to their leader.

"My brothers and sisters," he boomed, his voice echoing through the cavernous hall. "Too long have we suffered the indignities imposed upon us by those upstart Olympians."

Murmurs of discontent rippled through the crowd. Eyes narrowed. Jaws clenched. Oh yes, the thirst for vengeance ran deep. Cronus intended to tap into that bottomless well of rage.

"But no more!" He declared, pumping a mighty fist into the air. "The hour of destiny is upon us. Our informant tells us the Olympians have retreated to their stronghold on Mount

Olympus. The fools! Now is the time to strike, while they cower in their gilded cages."

More cheers erupted, along with the pounding of goblets on the table. The Titans were in a frenzy, bloodlust shining in their eyes.

Cronus nodded, gratified by their loyalty. The die was cast.

The revelry continued late into the night, the grand hall echoing with raucous laughter and drunken shouts. Servants scurried, refilling goblets of honeyed wine and heaping platters high with ambrosia, nectar, and the choicest roasts. They had spared no expense for Cronus's celebratory banquet.

In between courses, colorful troupes of dancers twirled and leaped gracefully to the music of lyres, pipes, and drums. Tale spitters regaled the guests with epic poems and rhyming couplets, while jesters cavorted about, drawing guffaws with their bawdy jokes and slapstick antics. Even the Muses joined in to sing and glorify the Titans.

As the night wore on, a sudden shriek pierced the din of merriment. Silence rippled outward as all eyes turned toward the source: Phoebe, daughter of Uranus, who had collapsed in the empty chair in a heap. Her slender frame trembled.

The goddess's silver-white hair flowed to her waist. The gown she wore was simple, with a girdle of gold around her waist. Her eyes were a gentle blue gray. A mystical prophet, she stood in the center of a light beam, brighter than the sun, and her skin and hair shone with the same light. Until now.

Cronus was on his feet in an instant, rushing to the aid of his older sister, the prophetic Titaness. "Speak, Phoebe! What did you see?"

She clutched at him with pale, trembling fingers. "A vision … a warning …" She gasped. "The Olympians … their weapons … forged by the cyclopes … terrible power …"

Uneasy murmurs spread through the hall. Cronus's jaw clenched, his hands balling into fists. After a moment, he whirled, bellowing for the music and revelry to continue. But unease lingered in every heart, Phoebe's chilling words haunting their thoughts.

Phoebe pleaded desperately, her voice trembling with urgency. "Cronus, have pity and save us all from certain destruction. I dreamed last night that the Olympians have powerful weapons. The world is theirs to rule now." She held her breath as she waited for an answer, her heart pounding like a hammer against her chest.

Cronos saw his wife Rhea's eyes pleading with him to understand Phoebe's words. She felt the strength of the Olympian gods surging through her veins, knowing they were now ready to crush their enemies and take victory in this war.

With a thunderous cry, Cronus erupted with anger. "No! I will never surrender! Not now, not ever!" His rage was clear in his face, more intense than the flames of Mount Olympus. He picked up his golden goblet and hurled it at his feet. Every shard that flew shone with fury.

Cronus forced a smile, though his eyes blazed. "Pay no heed to Phoebe's ramblings. The Olympians are no match for us."

He strode to the center of the hall, raising a new goblet high. "We, the Titans, have been ruling this world since the beginning of time. Have you forgotten? Our strength is absolute! No upstart gods could ever hope to challenge us."

His voice rose to a thunderous roar. "I won't surrender the throne to Poseidon and his family. I will crush the Olympians beneath our heels and remind them of their rightful place—groveling at our feet!"

The hall erupted with roars of approval and fists pounding on tables. Harsh laughter and shouts of "Death to the Olympians!" filled the air.

Inwardly, Cronus seethed, his thoughts racing. Phoebe's vision had unnerved him, though he dared not show it. The time of the Olympians was running out. He would see to it himself. Zeus's skull would adorn his throne before long.

This was only the beginning. Despite the upcoming battle, Cronus was determined to keep his power. Blood would flow, but in the end, the Titans would reign supreme.

The Titans feasted and drank wine and mead late into the night. Servants rushed, refilling goblets, and presenting an endless array of delicacies. Musicians played lively tunes, dancers twirled and leaped, and colorful lights lit up the grand hall.

At the center of it all sat Cronus, one arm draped lazily over his throne as he surveyed the festivities with a smug smile. He would fight to the death to keep his kingdom.

Suddenly, the braziers lining the walls flared bright red. Cronus bolted upright, eyes darting around the hall. Cries of alarm went up as the tapestries caught fire, the flames gorging the ancient fabrics.

"It's an omen!" someone shouted. "A sign from the gods!"

Cronus rose, face contorted in fury. "Curse the Olympians and my treacherous brothers, the cyclopes," Cronus thundered. "They dare threaten me in my hall?"

Then he spun around and grabbed his harpe, heading toward the banquet table. With swift grace, he cut through food, dishes, and glasses, sending them flying in suspended animation all around him. The red wine from the shattered glasses spread across the air and marble floor like spilled blood.

He kept going, destroying chairs and sofas with every swing of his blade. The Titans and guests ran for their lives as they scrambled away from Cronus's wrath. "This is what Olympians will become when we meet again," he yelled.

The Titan of Time stormed the palace, leaving an atmosphere of fear and destruction in his wake.

CHAPTER FIVE

THE SEA CHURNED VIOLENTLY, WAVES CRASHING AGAINST THE cliffs as Poseidon gazed out over the tumultuous waters. He felt burdened by the looming threat of Cronus. The Titans' desire for power put everyone at risk, including themselves and the Olympians. Poseidon knew the action must happen.

Gripping his mighty trident, Poseidon dove into the raging sea. The icy water embraced him as he propelled himself downward into the lightless depths. He spun and twisted, wielding the three-pronged spear with fluid skill. Thrusting and parrying, he mastered the trident's powers. He summoned massive waves and split boulders with devastating blows. The sea obeyed his every command.

Poseidon broke the surface, saltwater streaming down his powerful frame. He had honed his abilities well, but Cronus's forces were formidable. Could he defeat the Titans alone? The fate of the two worlds rested on his shoulders.

Jaw set with determination, Poseidon swam to shore. He would seek allies. United, they could end Cronus's dark reign. Poseidon refused to stand idle while Olympus fell.

The sea god stepped onto the beach, trident in hand. He was ready for the coming battle and would fight to protect all he held dear, no matter the cost.

Zeus's thunderous voice boomed, "Brother, wait!"

Poseidon turned to see Zeus descending from the heavens, electricity crackling around him. The sky god's piercing blue eyes were alight with purpose. "You do not standalone against Cronus," he declared. "I will fight by your side."

Hades emerged from billowing shadows, deathly pale and grim. "As will I," the underworld god rasped.

Poseidon clasped their shoulders, relief washing over him. "My brothers … thank you."

Together, they would be unstoppable. Poseidon's confidence swelled.

Zeus hefted his lightning bolt, testing its weight. "We must prepare. Hone our abilities for the coming battle."

Hades drew his wicked bident, its obsidian blade hungry for souls. "I will rally the dead to our cause."

Poseidon raised his trident into the sky. "And I will marshal the forces of the sea."

The brothers stood united, weapons at the ready. Cronus would regret the day he incurred their wrath. They would see the Titan's dark reign ended, no matter what the sacrifice required.

Poseidon met his brothers' determined gazes. The time had come.

He strode purposefully through the rocky tunnels, Zeus and Hades close behind. The air grew heavy with menace as they approached Cronus's inner sanctum. Poseidon tightened his grip on his trident, the weapon humming with power. He would need all his skills and magic to face what lay ahead.

Hades used his bident's powers to create a bridge between the Underworld and Mount Olympus, allowing the gods to cross over and battle Cronus.

Poseidon, Zeus, and Hades found the secret entrance to Cronus's lair.

They entered a vast cavern, shadows clinging to its edges. In the center loomed a massive obsidian throne, and upon it sat the hulking form of Cronus. The Titan's aura oozed malice, his stone-gray skin marred by pulsing purple veins. He turned, fixing the brothers with his malevolent amber eyes. "So, my wayward sons finally come to face their destiny," he rumbled. His voice echoed through the cavern, ancient and pitiless.

Poseidon stood firm, trident at the ready. "Your reign ends here, Titan."

Zeus and Hades fanned out on either side, lightning and death magic crackling from their weapons. United, they faced the dark king, undaunted by his powerful presence.

Cronus rose from his throne, the ground trembling beneath his footsteps. "You are fools to challenge me. I am eternal!" His words shook the cavern walls.

"No more!" Poseidon shouted, launching himself at his father, his brothers charging with him. The ultimate battle had begun.

Poseidon struck with all his might, determined to end Cronus's dark rule. Side by side with Zeus and Hades, they would triumph or fall together. The fate of the world now rested on their unity.

Poseidon's trident clashed against Cronus's massive scythe, sending sparks flying. The Titan was deceptively fast, parrying each of Poseidon's blows. Zeus flanked the left, hurling bolts of lightning that sizzled across Cronus's stony flesh. Hades slipped into the shadows, sending skeletal warriors to harry the Titan's feet.

Cronus roared, swinging his forceful scythe in a wide arc. Poseidon dove and rolled, narrowly avoiding decapitation. The Titan's strength was immense, each strike powerful enough to cleave stone.

"Is this the best you can muster, whelps?" Cronus taunted. His laughter echoed ominously throughout the cavern.

Poseidon's jaw clenched. He would not let the Titan shake their resolve. With a defiant cry, he summoned a crushing wall of water, slamming it into Cronus with the force of a tidal wave. The Titan staggered back under the aquatic onslaught.

"Now, brothers!" Poseidon yelled. Zeus rained lightning upon Cronus, while Hades's undead bident clawed at him. The Titan fell to one knee, ichor leaking from countless wounds.

Yet still he rose, eyes blazing. "You cannot defeat me. I am eternal!" Cronus battered them back, but the brothers regrouped. They would give everything to end the Titan's dark reign.

Poseidon gripped his trident, its power thrumming through him. Together, they charged once more. The fate of the world balanced on the edge of a blade.

Poseidon dove and weaved, avoiding the Titan's devastating blows. Cronus moved with astonishing speed for his size, centuries of battle honing his reflexes.

"Fight me, coward!" Cronus thundered. "Stop scurrying about like a rat!"

Poseidon's eyes narrowed. He feinted left, then rolled right, sweeping out with his trident. The prongs raked across Cronus's thigh, drawing a bellow of pain. Ichor splattered, sizzling where it struck stone.

From the shadows, Hades struck. Skeletal hands burst from the ground, grasping at Cronus's ankles. The Titan stomped and kicked, but still they clung.

"Wretched shades!" Cronus spat. "I will send you back to the pits of Tartarus!"

He smashed his fists down, obliterating Hades's minions. But the distraction provided the opening Zeus needed.

The sky god soared overhead, hands crackling with power. "Face the might of the heavens!" Zeus cried. Thunder boomed as he unleashed lightning in a blinding cascade. Bolts hammered Cronus like the fury of a hundred storms. The Titan spasmed violently, smoke rising from charred flesh.

Poseidon saw their chance. "Now, together!" Trident, thunderbolt, and bident cut into Cronus all at once. The Titan crumpled to his knees, ichor running in rivers.

"This cannot ... be," Cronus rasped. "I am ... eternal ..." His protestations faded as the light left his eyes.

The brothers had done it: Cronus was no more. They slumped in exhaustion, basking in their hard-won victory.

Hades released a bellow of rage that caused the mountain to tremble, reverberating throughout the darkness of the Underworld. His outstretched bident pierced into the pitch-black abyss as it opened the gates of hell to Tartarus.

The Olympians gathered their weapons with trepidation as Poseidon heaved his trident high in defiance. "Cronus, your reign, and the rule of the Titans are over! Your eternal punishment awaits you in the depths of Tartarus."

Hades, the God of Death, delivered a murderous thrust of his bident. Cronus's rag-doll body fell backward. Separated from his scythe, the god of time crashed into the fire of burning sulfur brimstone deep inside the bowels of Tartarus with an agonizing scream that rang through the darkness.

Poseidon leaned on his trident, chest heaving. The battle had taken everything he had, but the results spoke for themselves. Cronus lay broken at their feet, finally defeated after eons of tyranny.

A rumbling sound came from the earth itself as the foundations of Cronus's empire trembled. Cracks spread like a spider-web across the ground, and walls crumbled. It was as if the very world was reacting to the Titan's demise.

Hades rested a comforting hand on Poseidon's shoulder. "It's over, brother. We are free."

Zeus wiped ichor from his thunderbolt as he surveyed the decimated battlefield. "The age of the Titans has ended. Now begins the reign of the Olympians."

Poseidon nodded wearily. After so long under Cronus's heel, freedom was almost beyond imagination. Yet, as he looked at his brothers, Poseidon felt hope. United, they had accomplished what none could alone. The future lay open before them.

"Come," said Zeus. "Let us leave this place of death. Work remains for a new world to be built."

The brothers turned their backs on the broken form of Cronus. Their alliance had reshaped destiny itself. The promise of a better era was clear in their eyes as they walked into the sunlight. The age of gods and mortals had begun.

CHAPTER SIX

THE ACRID SMOKE STILL HUNG HEAVY OVER THE BATTLEFIELD AS Poseidon surveyed the smoldering ruins of the underworld of Mount Olympus. The scars of war remained on the land, despite their victory over Cronus. Poseidon's eyes narrowed with determination as his brothers joined him atop the cliff.

"It is time," Zeus declared, his voice booming like thunder over the desolate valley. "We must rebuild this world that our father sought to destroy."

The battle won over the Titans, Rhea, mother of the Olympians, welcomed her victorious children into the magnificent palace on Mount Olympus. Wearing a blue tunic bejeweled with gold braid around her waist, her red, braided hair glorified with golden threads, she looked radiant.

As the warriors entered the dining hall, Rhea greeted them with overflowing platters of food and barrels filled with wine. "Let us celebrate your triumph! Sit and recount your story."

Poseidon, Hades, and Zeus trudged in exhaustion to the table laden with food and drink. While they feasted, the trio shared their heroic tales of their daring battle against their deceptive father, Cronus.

When the Olympians had eaten, Rhea pulled a golden bowl from the center of the table. The moment of truth has arrived to determine the ruler of each part of the world and the king of all. Shocked, the Olympians looked at one another. None had expected such division. Only their mother, who married their tyrant father and their champion, conducted the ritual, as it was fair.

Rhea lifted her arm gracefully above her head while grasping three jet-black tokens engraved with unknowable symbols within them. "The Fates have blessed these lots for your guidance. Select one, and it will reveal your destiny."

She held out the golden basin so high that none could see inside it as she commanded each warrior to dip his right hand into its depths and take one lot.

"The seas and waters shall be yours, Poseidon," Rhea proclaimed. "To nurture life and create new lands and growth wherever your waves may reach."

Poseidon nodded, though uncertainty still stirred in his heart. He gazed out at the gray, tumultuous ocean, feeling the pull of its mysterious depths.

Rhea turned to Hades. His piercing black eyes alight. "Lord of the Underworld, the dead shall live in your domain."

Hades's pallid face remained impassive, obsidian eyes betraying nothing. He would rule the realm in solitude and shadow, ever loyal to his family, despite his isolated fate.

Rhea, tears in her eyes, turned to Zeus. "The heavens and sky are yours, my son. And because of your bravery to free your siblings and ensure the freedom from the Titans, you will also rule as the rightful king of gods and mortals."

Poseidon bristled, the sea raging in tandem with the storm in his heart. But he held his tongue for now, the injustice brewing bitterly as gall within him.

He was prepared to challenge his brother's rule. For now, he kept his own counsel, his desires as unfathomable as the ocean's depths.

Poseidon turned and surveyed the shimmering expanse of the sea. The tang of salt hung in the air as waves crashed against the shore, sea foam swirling around his feet.

This domain would be his to master, to shape as he saw fit. His weathered hands flexed as he imagined the creatures he could create, beasts that would prowl the ocean's shadowy depths and guard its treasures. Mysteries awaited him in those uncharted waters.

Poseidon waded into the surf, the icy waves invigorating him. He would explore every cove and trench, build splendid palaces beneath the waves. None could challenge him here.

Looking back at the towering figures of Zeus and Hades on the beach, he felt a twinge of regret. They had stood together against Cronus, but already fractures split their bond.

Poseidon dove beneath the surface, powerful limbs propelling him through the murky water. He would bide his time and gather his strength. When the day came to confront Zeus, the sea would rise to his command.

For now, he lost himself in the current's restless pull. The ocean welcomed its new master as he delved into its secrets, his desire for independence as boundless as the sea.

Poseidon emerged from the depths, saltwater streaming down his muscular frame as he strode onto the beach. In the distance, he could see Zeus standing atop Mount Olympus, thunderclouds gathering around him. Poseidon's eyes flashed with anger at the sight.

He had not forgotten how their mother's favorite son, Zeus, with her proclamation, would hold dominion over the world and the skies. Poseidon clenched his fists, rage simmering within him. He thought his might and strength, like his father's, gave him the ability to rule, only to have Zeus snatch that right from him.

Sand swirled around Poseidon's feet, reacting to the intensity of his emotions. The sea churned in sympathy with its master's turmoil.

How dare Zeus presume to rule the world? We should have ruled together as equals. Instead, Zeus was king while relegating Poseidon to the waves and shadows.

I have all the water and its creatures. The dead of the world belong to Hades forever. And Zeus gets to be king.

Jaw tightening, Poseidon strode back into the surf until he was waist deep. The cool water helped calm the anger burning through his veins. He would bide his time … for now.

Poseidon lifted his trident, feeling its power thrumming in his hands. One day he would remind Zeus what he could command with a strike of this weapon—tidal waves tall as mountains, maelstroms that could swallow navies whole.

When that day came, Zeus would realize his mistake. The seas bow to no one. And neither would Poseidon.

Poseidon's knuckles whitened as he gripped his trident, the metal creaking under the pressure. With a snarl, he turned and stalked out of the waves, his footprints burning into glass in the sand.

"I will not kneel at your feet, brother," Poseidon growled under his breath. "You claim dominion over this world, but your reach is limited," he retorted. "The seas are mine to rule, now and forever. Test me at your peril."

The roaring ocean swallowed his words, but Poseidon knew Zeus would hear them soon enough. Let the thunderer sit atop his mountain and watch the storms gather on the horizon. Poseidon's realm was vast and wild, impossible to tame.

With a rush of power, Poseidon summoned a wave to carry him away from the shore. The cresting water bore him swiftly over the open ocean as schools of fish darted out of his way. The familiar roll of the sea calmed his anger, letting his mind clear.

What use was rage when patience and cunning would serve him better? Poseidon was no fool. Directly challenging Zeus would gain him nothing. But the oceans hid endless secrets beneath their waves. In time, Poseidon would discover how to shift the tides in his favor.

For now, he would explore the breadth of his dominion. The sea welcomed its rightful master. And soon, Zeus would come to understand the folly of believing he could control forces beyond his reach.

Poseidon dove beneath the surface, reveling in the muted hush of the underwater world. The gods' politics were inconsequential down here.

As he swam deeper, the sunlight filtering through the water faded to an inky blackness. Strange creatures lurked in these hidden depths, monsters, and wonders unseen by mortal eyes. Poseidon studied them with curiosity, noting their powers and potential weaknesses.

One beast gave him pause: a massive leviathan with rows of razor-sharp teeth. Its size rivaled the Titan Cronus himself. Yet it bowed its majestic head in deference as Poseidon approached, recognizing its master.

Poseidon rested a hand on the leviathan's snout, a plan already forming. He wouldn't need to challenge Zeus directly with these titanic creatures under his command. At the right moment, Poseidon would rise from the sea and shake Olympus.

Patience and cunning, he reminded himself. Poseidon smiled, savoring the thought of the thunderer's surprise when the ocean's depths revealed their secrets. The sea god's reign had just started.

Poseidon returned to the surface. His anger toward Zeus momentarily subsided as he contemplated the forces stirring in the deep. They quickly reignited his wrath.

He strode along the shoreline, his fists clenched. How dare Zeus presume dominion over him? Had they not all played a part in overthrowing Cronus?

Poseidon recalled with bitterness the moment he had drawn the lot, assigning him lordship of the seas. A paltry consolation compared to the skies and Mount Olympus.

"One day, brother, you will regret underestimating me," Poseidon growled under his breath. The waves crashed higher in response to his fury. "Well, at least I can create new lands. Even Zeus cannot do that."

Thunder rumbled in the distance, as if Zeus accepted the challenge. Poseidon's lip curled in a sneer. Let the posturing begin. Their battle would be epic, but Poseidon had eons to develop his plans.

For now, he would walk among mortals to seek allies. Dissatisfied individuals would support Poseidon over Zeus. A kingdom could not stand without loyal subjects.

Poseidon's stride became purposeful as he moved inland, away from the sea. The time gathered his strength and let darkness work its subtle influence. When the moment arrived to unleash the ocean's wrath, Poseidon would be ready.

Olympus gods underestimated the power of the deep, leading to regret. This, Poseidon vowed.

PART TWO

POSEIDON'S ATLANTIS ADVENTURE

THE HUMAN HYBRID EXPERIMENT

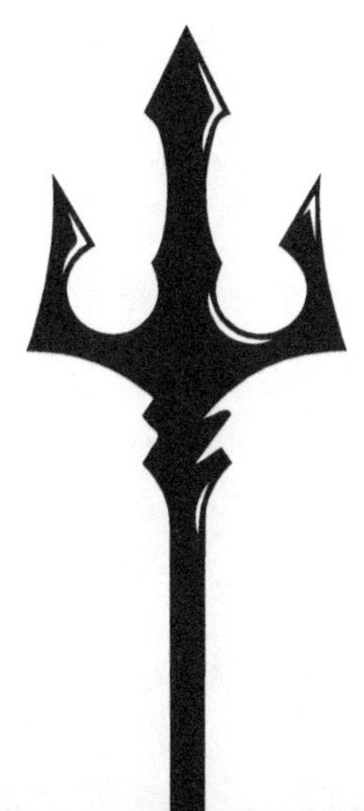

CHAPTER SEVEN
15,600 B.C.

POSEIDON SWAM THROUGH THE DEPTHS OF AZURE-BLUE WATERS, his trident crackling with power. Fish scattered and manta rays parted before him, as if sensing his ancient fury roiling beneath the surface. He reached out, grasping a manta ray in one hand, feeling its leathery skin bumping against his fingers.

The sea creatures were an unwelcome comfort; man, and god alike, had forgotten him. Now he felt only bitterness and isolation in this lonesome kingdom of shadows beneath the waves. "What is my purpose?" he snarled, lightning bolts sparking from his trident as he spoke. The fish fled, leaving only silence in their wake.

With a flick of his trident, Poseidon propelled himself upward, breaching the surface. A bath of foam exploded. The sun blinded him for a moment, its reflection rippling atop the waves. Poseidon blinked, then turned his gaze to the horizon.

He plunged through the depths of the sea, feeling a thrill at the icy embrace that welcomed him. Schools of fish fled in terror before him as he pierced through the water with his trident, sending clouds of sand into the air. Anemones swayed and tentacles unfurled to reach their microscopic prey. Poseidon shivered in delight at the sight.

A pair of dolphins materialized beside him, chirping, and beckoning him to play. He let out a low chuckle as he followed their graceful movements, spinning and twirling amid the crystalline waters. They lifted a burden from his shoulders, and he enjoyed his domain.

He noticed a whale breaching in the distance, its humped back shining against the filtered sunlight. With every passing stroke, Poseidon drew closer until he reached out and ran his fingertips along its barnacled skin.

The whale seemed to accept him without judgment or demands. Here, Poseidon felt accepted, and he swam onward with a newfound purpose.

Yet though he held dominion over the wide expanse of the sea, Poseidon could not escape the suffocating sense of betrayal that lingered within him. Zeus had cast him aside, relegating him to the depths, and had kept Olympus to himself. Poseidon was indignant, as Zeus did not consider the sea as an equal, despite its being the cradle of life.

Poseidon sunk into his ornate throne, crafted from coral and adorned with pearls. This was his kingdom, yet it felt like a prison of solitude. Poseidon glanced up through the arched windows at the sunlight rippling far above—the surface world where his divine siblings now reigned supreme.

In the past, Poseidon commanded reverence and awe. Things had changed, and he'd felt purposeless again. A deep sorrow filled his heart as Poseidon wrestled with despair.

What was his destiny, according to the Fates? What was his new role? The answers eluded him, as murky and unfathomable as the ocean depths.

Poseidon clenched his trident, its golden prongs glinting. Though his power had waned, he was still a force to be reckoned with. He needed to remind others of his power and shake Olympus's foundations.

But how? And to what end? The questions churned within Poseidon like a maelstrom. For now, they remained unanswered.

Poseidon rose from his throne and swam through the open arched windows, leaving his palace behind. He moved through the blue-green waters, the sea creatures scattering before their lord.

As he swam, memories of the distant past surfaced in Poseidon's mind. He recalled walking the earth in his full glory during the Golden Age of the Titans before Zeus cast him down. Back then, the mortals had worshipped the gods, built grand temples and making rich offerings. How vividly Poseidon remembered processions of robed priests leading bulls garlanded with flowers to be sacrificed in his name. The smoke rising heavenward, carrying his praises.

Those days were long gone. Human perception had turned gods into myths and legends, and relegated Poseidon to the silent depths, his only companions the fish that darted around him.

After ages, Poseidon desired the sun and wind. To experience the crash of waves on the shore. A brief visit to the surface world was possible. To recall the feeling of being revered, take a walk on land.

He tilted his head back, gazing up at the rippling light far above. Yes, he would ascend and reacquaint himself with the earthly realm again. He must be careful, as Zeus wouldn't approve of him being on land. It must be a brief visit.

With powerful strokes, Poseidon swam upward, ready to breach the surface. He broke through, feeling the sun's rays on his skin for the first time in decades. The warmth invigorated him, filling him with a vitality he had not known since the days of sacrifices and prayers.

He scanned the horizon, looking for signs of life on the nearby island. In the distance, he could make out the shapes of buildings along the coastline. A harbor bustling with ships and people.

As he swam closer, flashes of memory surfaced in Poseidon's mind. Laughing maidens dancing along the shore, offering wreaths of flowers. Bronze braziers burning, sending the smell of roasted meat and incense into the air. He could almost hear the cries of adoration from throngs of worshippers.

But as he drew near the island's edge, Poseidon saw no wreaths or braziers. No throngs lined up to praise him. The ships in the harbor flew flags and banners he did not recognize. He heard sailors shouting in an unfamiliar language.

Poseidon's heart sank. This was no longer his domain. The changing world had left him behind. All that remained of his glorious past were myths and legends.

He watched the sailors go about their work, loading cargo and mending nets. So focused on their mundane tasks. Oblivious to the god staring at them from just offshore.

With a flick of his mighty trident, Poseidon turned away. He no longer belonged in the surface world. Sea creatures would give him purpose in the silent depths. They, at least, still treated him with reverence.

As the sunlight faded behind him, Poseidon descended into the cool darkness of his underwater kingdom. Acceptance had replaced the longing in his heart. This was where he belonged now.

Poseidon swam deeper into the ocean, leaving the island and its unfamiliar inhabitants behind. The rays of sunlight faded as he entered the midnight zone.

Strange bioluminescent creatures glimmered in the surrounding darkness. Poseidon reached out a hand and caressed a passing lantern fish. Its light brightened at his divine touch.

Though the ocean's residents still revered him, Poseidon felt disconnected from this realm. He had been in control of marine life for ages, but a subtle change was occurring.

The sea creatures behaved more erratically in his presence. Their communication became garbled and confused, as if his very divinity disturbed them. Poseidon pondered what the change meant.

In the distance, a shadow moved. Poseidon swam toward it, his godly senses detecting a massive creature ahead. As it came into view, he saw it was a giant squid, larger than any he'd encountered before.

The squid's tentacles lashed out, its eyes wild and frenzied. Poseidon raised his trident, ready to subdue the maddened beast. But he hesitated, sensing this was no ordinary animal. A sinister intelligence lurked within it.

The squid fixed its savage gaze upon Poseidon. In its abyssal voice, it spoke a single word: "Hecate."

Poseidon recoiled in dismay. The cult! They had reached even these lightless depths. A profound unease filled him, along with a renewed sense of purpose.

The challenges ahead would be great. But Poseidon resolved that no matter what darkness lay in wait, he would regain his rightful place in this changing world. For now, he still had dominion here.

With a roar, Poseidon surged forward, his trident gleaming.

CHAPTER EIGHT

POSEIDON STOOD ALONE ATOP THE CLIFFS; HIS GAZE FIXED upon the endless sea. The crashing waves and crying gulls were deaf to the turmoil in his heart. How far he had fallen from the glory of his youth. Once, kings bowed and nations trembled at the mere whisper of his name. He was now just a fading memory.

The taste of betrayal still burned on his tongue. His divine family's petty schemes had caused his downfall, not mortal hubris. Zeus, ever jealous of his power, had schemed with his mother, Rhea, and others, like his niece Artemis, to undermine him. They had succeeded, bit by bit, until all that remained of Poseidon's dominion were scraps of faith clinging to life in forgotten fishing villages.

Poseidon clenched his fist. No, he would not fade into obscurity. He would reclaim what they had stolen from him. The sea god's eyes turned away with new fire. To unlock forgotten secrets and powers, an ancient journey was necessary.

"I swear by the rivers Styx and Titan, by the primal sea whence I sprang, I shall have my glory again," Poseidon vowed. His words seemed to stir the tides themselves, waves crashing louder in answer.

Yes, he would voyage deep into the heart of mystery. He would brave the darkest depths and scale the highest peaks. And when he returned, woe to any who stood in his way. The era of Poseidon would begin anew.

Poseidon made his way to a secluded grotto hidden from mortal eyes. This place held an energy unlike anywhere else on earth, a tinge of power that prickled the skin. Perfect for the rituals ahead.

First, he drew a circle of smoldering ash and crushed bone upon the stone floor. Then, opening a leather pouch at his side, he retrieved a vial of kraken ink, pouring it to form strange sigils and runes within the circle's bounds. While pouring the vial of kraken ink, Poseidon uttered words in the old tongue.

The air grew heavy, charged with gathering power. The sigils began to glow, pulsing in time with Poseidon's incantations. He raised his arms high, fixing his will upon the spell circle. This ritual was one of summoning, of calling forth a majestic beast from the dawn of time.

There was a crack like thunder as the spell circle flared bright. When the glare faded, an astonishing sight met Poseidon's eyes. Before him reared a mighty hippocampus, scales glimmering like rainbows on the sea. It whinnied, pawing the air with its front hooves.

Poseidon allowed himself a smile. Here was a companion fitting for the journeys ahead. He approached, stroking the hippocampus's mane. It nuzzled him in return, sensing a bond between god and beast.

"Together, we shall travel where no god has set foot for eons beyond count," Poseidon said. The hippocampus neighed in answer. Their pact was now sealed. "We begin the voyage into shadow and legend." Poseidon's quest to reclaim his glory had begun at last.

Poseidon gazed at the magnificent, gigantic seahorse one last time, then turned to gather supplies for the impending journey. He packed, bringing only what was necessary—a satchel of ambrosia and nectar, a map of the forgotten realms, and his mighty trident.

His thoughts turned to those he was leaving behind. Though gods were immortal, partings still carried poignancy. Poseidon thought of his son Triton, a merman, half man and half fish, who he would miss the most. They had parted ways, still nursing the wounds of past arguments. Perhaps when he returned, things would mend between them.

"I shall return if the Fates allow it," Poseidon murmured. With a heavy sigh, he turned toward the waiting hippocampus. It was time to depart the familiar shores of the Aegean for the unknown. He mounted up, taking hold of the hippocampus's flowing mane.

Poseidon paused, casting one last look over glittering waves and white columns. Although diminished, this remained his domain. The majesty of ages past called to him from beyond the horizon.

"Onward!" he cried, and the hippocampus reared before diving into the surf. Their figures diminished as they raced over swells and into the rising sun.

The hippocampus swam with astonishing speed, its scales glinting as it cut through the waves. Poseidon bent low, relishing the sea spray on his face. How long had it been since he traversed the open ocean like this? Too long.

In the distance, storm clouds gathered, rumbling with thunder. The winds picked up, whipping the sea into a froth. Poseidon narrowed his eyes. His brother Zeus must know of his quest. The storm warned to turn back.

"Faster!" Poseidon urged the hippocampus. It complied, muscles rippling as it streamed forward. Lightning cracked overhead, striking close. Still, they raced on. A towering wave reared before them. Poseidon gripped the hippocampus as it dove straight through the thundering crest.

They burst out on the other side. The wave crashing down behind them. Poseidon let out a defiant laugh. *Try harder, brother!*

The ocean seethed as more waves and wind buffeted them. Still, Poseidon would not turn back. A strange light glowed beneath the surface before them. The hippocampus balked, letting out a shrill cry.

"Steady now," Poseidon said, stroking its mane. The glow intensified, revealing itself as a whirlpool. Dark and swirling, it yawned wider, beckoning them closer. Poseidon set his jaw. This was no force of nature, but magic meant to impede him.

"Take us through," he told the hippocampus. Trusting its master's command, the beast plunged into the maelstrom's depths. Down and down they spun, the roar deafening. Poseidon clung fast, the forces threatening to rip him away.

With a final gut-wrenching surge, they burst forth into calm waters. Poseidon's laugh echoed over the still sea. "Well done, my friend!" The first trial was past. More lay ahead, but Poseidon's resolve only grew. He would reclaim his glory, no matter the cost.

Poseidon stroked the hippocampus's neck as they glided through the tranquil waters. Yet despite overcoming the whirlpool, a lingering unease still gripped him. This journey was necessary, but doubts crept in.

Had he acted, letting pride blind him? The sea no longer bowed to his will alone. Though it pained him, sharing dominion was perhaps prudent. The world had changed much since his reign began. New gods, new mortals, walked the earth. Their reverence waned as the old ways faded.

Poseidon sighed, gazing at his reflection on the glassy surface. He recognized the face staring back—wearied, aged.

In the distance, a hazy island emerged. Poseidon approached, half-eager, half-apprehensive at what he might find there.

The hippocampus glided to a stop near the crumbling docks, sensing its master's hesitation. Poseidon steeled himself and dismounted. This place held answers about his past and his future path. With purposeful steps, he walked ashore.

CHAPTER NINE

THE OCEAN'S ROAR FILLED POSEIDON'S EARS AS HE STRODE ACROSS the pristine beach, his feet sinking into the ivory sand with each step. The waves crashed and foamed before him in an endless rhythm, the azure waters glittering under the high sun. For a moment he paused, breathing in the briny air, a sense of peace washing over him.

Further down the beach, a young woman glided along the tide line, her gaze cast downward as she collected seashells in a woven basket. Her skin glowed golden in the sunlight, complementing her long blonde hair that cascaded down her back in gentle waves. She wore a simple white chiton, cinched at the waist with a braided belt.

Poseidon watched her, curiosity stirring within him. There was something familiar in the way she moved, her bare feet leaving fleeting impressions on the damp sand. She appeared to be connected to this shore. His brow furrowed. Who was she?

Poseidon's gaze followed every graceful movement as she moved across his domain. Smitten by her beauty, and with curiosity about who this ethereal being was, appearing upon his shores. His heart warmed at the sight of this wondrous creature, who had arrived from somewhere beyond his ken. Infatuated by an unexpected surge of lighthearted excitement, he drew closer to see if he could discern where she came from and how she had gained such an incredible glow.

The young maiden couldn't believe her eyes as she watched an enormous man climb out of the ocean, his black hair cascading down his face like waves and seaweed adorning his powerful body. Fear struck in her heart as he stepped forward, but his beauty and grace transfixed her. His deadly trident glinted in the sun, and she wondered what such a mighty weapon meant for her.

Poseidon's voice is gentle yet demanding. "Who are you? What brings you here?"

Her reply was soft and melodic. "I am Cleito, daughter of Euenor and Leucippus, who live here on this island. And who are you?"

The gentle giant and Cleito's eyes met. The god of the sea smiled. "I am Poseidon." He put his hand on his heart and bowed. He stared at her for a moment longer, disbelief written across his features.

Poseidon's eyes widened when he heard "Leucippus." He wondered if it could be the same young water nymph he had once known. She, along with her sisters, were companions of Persephone when Hades had abducted the damsel.

"Wait." He tried to stop her from leaving him by the sea. "Let me wash this seaweed from my blair." He picked up his trident and bounded into the water, throwing off a shawl of seaweed in an instant that cloaked his body like a warm embrace. A rivulet of water snaked down his leg as it splashed into the tide behind him. The sun glistened on his golden trident, a testament to his power. After washing away the remnants of the sea's embrace, he stuck his trident deep into the sand.

The thought lingered in his mind. Curiosity led him onward, and with each step toward Cleito, he approached not only her but also the possibility of a connection that transcended time.

As she watched him approach unarmed, Cleito's heart began to thump as she realized something was about to change. She urged, "Come meet my family; I can tell you will be welcome!"

Poseidon relaxed at the invitation. "Let me retrieve my trident. It will help me protect you and your family."

They walked up the trail together, leaving the sandy shore behind and entering a realm of vibrant foliage and mystical energy. A lush canopy of towering trees seemed to reach out with curious branches and painted the landscape with an array of colors.

Jasmine and gardenia grew in abundance, lacing the air with floral scents, while meandering Andara crystals glowed from within, infused with life-giving properties that enhanced their beauty.

High above, tropical birds with feathers that shone like pearls soared through the sky. The calls of marlinspikes, parrots, and bosun birds filled the air, an orchestral symphony that echoed through the woodland—a living testament to the harmony of nature.

Within just a few paces, Poseidon's steps faltered as he neared his goal. His chest tightened at the sight before him: Cleito had just emerged from a copse of brush. Emotions surged through him as he gazed into her familiar yet strange eyes.

"Why am I so joyful? I am tingling all over." His eyes widened with pleasure as he noticed the hair on his arms standing up.

Cleito smiled as she turned to the giant man, whose eyes glowed with delight. "Our paradise sits on one of the planet's ley lines of cosmic energy that make up the Earth's electromagnetic field. The landmass rests on a spiraling force that raises the vibration of the earth. High energy helps balance the chakras of our bodies, keeping us healthier."

She pointed out the large crystals scattered across the grass. "Look at the Andara. These are high-frequency crystals from a distant galaxy. Each color has its own healing frequency. They like the high vortex of the soil and grow here."

Cleito described her home as they approached. It was a four-thousand-eight-hundred-square-mile paradise of emerald valleys, mountains, spires, and cliffs. Its varied climates ranged from humid tropical to subarctic. Her magical home jutted out over a ridge overlooking the sea with a cobalt-blue rooftop made of lava mix. The three-thousand-four-hundred-square-foot, four-sided structure could withstand earthquakes and hurricanes, and well insulated.

Her father, Euenor, glanced out the open wooden shutters to see his daughter walking toward home with a visitor. In his fifties and seven feet in height, his white hair hung in long locks over his muscular, tanned shoulders. A short beard gave him a regal presence. He wore a red smock with the seal of a golden eight-star crest that covered his belted, white, knee-length tunic. He smiled at the young couple. His piercing blue eyes matched his daughter's.

The patriarch called to his wife, Leucippus. "Come here. I can't talk to you without your dear face close to mine."

Laughing at her husband's antics, she wiped her hands on a cloth before the meal and sat across from him so that he could hold her hands and look into her eyes. She wore a floor-length white linen dress tied around the waist with a cotton ribbon. A pale-yellow tassel dangled off the end of each tie knot. In her mid-forties now, silver strands wove through her blonde hair, which was pulled into a bun on top of her head. Her smile was bright when she saw Cleito walking home with Poseidon and waved to them inside.

Leu threw her hand across her mouth. "Oh, my gosh! It's Poseidon!"

The front mahogany door opened. Cleito casually entered with Poseidon, as if it were normal to drop in for dinner with an uninvited guest.

Poseidon marched through the threshold behind Cleito and had to duck under the doorway lintel to get inside of the roomy house with large windows for light and air flow. Leucippus's presence startled the sea god.

He smiled. "White Horse, is that you? What happened to you after your abduction and the rescue that happened with Hades?"

Cleito's mother blushed. Her lips arched into a broad smile and her cheeks reddened like a morning glory. She moved back in amazement to see the god of the sea, Poseidon.

"Mother, do you know this man?" Cleito asked, to which her mother slowly nodded. "I met him many years ago. But please, won't you invite him in?"

Euenor's brow knitted at the surprising exchange. How did his wife know this stranger? "So, tell us, Leu. How do you know him?"

Leucippus rushed out of the room. "I smell our midday meal burning." Her daughter went after her into the kitchen.

Standing next to Leu, she asked, "Mother, please tell me. How do you know Poseidon?"

Meanwhile, in the dining area, the tension between Euenor and Poseidon turned awkward. Avoiding interaction, each man's eyes ping-ponged back and forth.

Poseidon lowered his voice and mumbled, "Let us wait for Leucippus. She will reveal how we are familiar. I do not want any misunderstandings."

Fragrant, fresh snapper, sautéed spinach, and fruit wafted into the dining room as Leucippus and Cleito brought in each dish to sit on the oval, acacia wood table. Nervous energy filled the room as Cleito began to pass the dishes around the table.

Poseidon raised his head to glimpse Leucippus turning shades of red. When each person had filled their plate, she cleared her throat and spoke in a trembling voice. "I connect my bloodline to Poseidon's family. Your father knows that at one time, I was a water nymph. A long time ago, my sisters and I were companions of Persephone. Hades, the God of the Underworld, abducted her. When Poseidon came to rescue us, he saw my strength and purity of heart and named me White Horse, or Leucippus."

"It was a proud moment for me. However, Poseidon, being a god, turned me into a mortal. Anyone who has been around gods long enough knows it's agony. I have not shared this story because it might sound strange. It was a painful memory."

Poseidon reached across the table to touch Leucippus's hand. "I am so sorry for what happened to you and your sisters. You were brave. Your heart was fervent, so I wanted to honor you with the proper name, White Horse, and allow you to live a life with the promise of a family." With damp eyes, he said, "And I see you have wonderful loved ones!"

Euenor's jaw dropped in shock as his wife told her incredible story. She'd descended from the god of the sea! He remembered when he had first noticed her. She was a water nymph, which he never thought was possible. Her agelessness amazed him over the years.

Cleito's eyes shone with delight, and her smile widened as the news began to sink in. "Wow, Mom, what a secret you have been keeping from us all these years! We would never have known, had Poseidon not washed up on our shores."

Poseidon regarded Leucippus and gave her a small compliment before leaning in closer, brushing away a wisp of hair from her face. "Your daughter didn't back away in fear when I appeared before her on the beach. She stood and welcomed me into your home as if it were mine, too. Cleito and you share a unique strength of character."

Leucippus felt a deep shudder ripple through her body as the truth of her secret escaped her lips. The weight of it lifted, but she feared what judgment her husband and Cleito would show her later. Taking hasty steps away from them, she stormed out of the dining room, needing space to think and fume.

Cleito cleared the table, leaving Poseidon and Euenor alone. Euenor motioned for Poseidon to follow him. Together they walked toward the outdoor spa set in the center of the patio. A stunning fountain stood tall in the middle of the yard with spring water pouring over ten tiers of enormous leaf petals that glinted in the light, reflecting from Andara crystals embedded within them. The tranquility of bubbling water surged into a twenty-foot pool, inviting both men to take a seat near its edge.

Euenor pulled two high-backed, rattan chairs close to them as dusk began to settle in, painting the sky a lush blend of pastel pink, indigo, and lavender hues.

Poseidon sat, unsure what to expect in this unfamiliar home. He could feel the tension between himself and Euenor. He cleared his throat. "Thank you for having me here. Your family is lovely. I want to reassure you that my association with your wife is distant. She has remarkable abilities with animals and water creatures."

Euenor chuckled at Poseidon's remark. "Yes, I have seen her work wonders with fish. They converse like old friends! We met in Greece when she was but a young girl, like Cleito."

Before Euenor could speak further, an uncomfortable silence ensued.

Euenor motioned toward a bedroom near them. "Please stay with us for a while; make yourself at home. I will speak with my wife and Cleito about it. Would you like that?"

The god of the sea hesitated. Though curious about this paradise, his heart still yearned for his past life and Greece. He debated and stayed.

"Good. I want to take you into the mountains tomorrow," Euenor said. "I will reveal the story behind this paradise to you. Let me introduce you to someone. Now get some rest. I am going to bed. I rise early to watch the sunrise. Let's convene in the dining room. We will have a light breakfast before we leave."

Poseidon closed his eyes, trying to feel peace despite his apprehension. The stars were shining above him, yet he felt distant from them. A light breeze wafted through the flora and fauna. Despite the parrot's squawk and the night creatures' songs, Poseidon trudged back to the cottage. Even after going to bed, he couldn't sleep because of conflicting emotions.

CHAPTER TEN

Poseidon, sleepless, rose from his bed and took a walk. While walking, he discovered Cleito at the edge of the rocky outcropping. The sea crashed against the cliffs far below. The salty spray misted his face as he approached.

Poseidon was struck by Cleito's regal beauty. Her long, blonde hair whipped in the sea breeze as she gazed pensively at the breathtaking panorama. Though young, Cleito exuded an aura of wisdom beyond her years.

"What brings you here?" Poseidon's resonant voice echoed across the cliffs.

Cleito met the sea god's intense, sea-green eyes. "Our people suffered without ancestral wisdom for too long." She gestured to the sprawling metropolis in the valley below, its magnificent temples and towers glinting in the dying light.

"Here lie the secrets of the ages. Ancient technology to elevate us beyond our mortal constraints." Her voice rang with conviction. "But the way forward remains obscured. Only with your divine intellect can we unravel the mysteries of this realm and usher in a new, enlightened era."

Poseidon stroked his bearded chin, contemplating her words. This was an unexpected development. When he had first encountered Cleito, she had seemed but a simple island girl. Now her quest resonated with his own desire to regain his former standing among the gods.

Perhaps their goals intertwined. If he could help her achieve hers, she might aid him in his. This land held promise and peril in equal measure. But wisdom without challenge was stagnation.

"Very well, Cleito," he declared. "We shall see what secrets this island holds."

Poseidon followed Cleito along the rocky coastal path, the cries of exotic birds and the roar of the surf filling his ears. Despite the unfamiliar land, the sea creature found comfort in the salt air.

Cleito led him through a narrow ravine carved into the cliffs, the shadows deepening as the last light faded from the sky. Poseidon conjured an orb of pale fire to light their way, noting how Cleito startled at this casual display of power. The ravine opened into a sheltered valley, the massive bulk of a stepped pyramid looming before them in the magical light.

Cleito turned to him, her eyes alight. "Behold, here lies the wisdom of the Ancients, yet its doors remain sealed. But with you, my lord, we can unlock its secrets."

Poseidon regarded the edifice, intrigued by the alien architecture and the intricate carvings adorning its facade. He felt a powerful resonance in this place, but wasn't sure what it was. "How do you propose we unveil its mysteries?" he asked.

Before Cleito could respond, a stern voice cut through the darkness. "She does not know, Poseidon. That is why I summoned you here."

Euenor emerged from the shadows. His long white hair and beard contrasted with his otherwise youthful features and piercing silver eyes. He wore a simple robe, yet carried himself with an air of authority that piqued the sea god's interest.

Euenor greeted his guest. "Welcome to our realm, son of Cronus." His gaze was penetrating. "I know why you have come. But the answers you seek live here, not in the world above."

Poseidon's eyes narrowed. "Euenor? I did not expect to see you until tomorrow morning. Your being here is a surprise." Even as his curiosity deepened. How did this mortal discern his hidden motives? There was depth to him beyond what was visible.

Much more.

Poseidon bristled at the mortal's presumptuous tone. "You claim to know my mind, Euenor? Speak, then. What answers do you believe I seek?"

Poseidon observed Euenor was unperturbed by the sea god's show of temper. He clasped his hands behind his back and began pacing before the towering edifice. "You seek confirmation of your true lineage, do you not? You wish to understand the source of your godly abilities. And why did your father, Cronus, see fit to overthrow his own sire."

The words struck Poseidon like a physical blow. How could this man divine his deepest doubts and insecurities? Unease stirred within him even as his pride rebelled. "My lineage is no concern of yours, mortal," he snapped.

Euenor raised a placating hand. "Peace, Poseidon. I do not judge you. The Ancients hold the answer. If you would claim your rightful heritage, you must open your mind to new truths."

Poseidon hesitated, pride warring with curiosity.

Sensing his conflict, Euenor pressed on. "We stand before the Font of Knowledge. Drink from the Font of Knowledge," he said, "and it will clarify everything. But I warn you, the enlightenment it offers can be … unsettling. Will you brave the revelations within?"

Poseidon stared at the imposing edifice, his mind racing. His desire to comprehend the secrets of his divine heritage had been aroused by Euenor's words.

Drawing himself up, he turned to Cleito and Euenor. "I accept your challenge. Lead on."

The sea god would brave any turbulence to grasp the truth of his lineage. The Font's secrets beckoned, and he would answer their call.

Cleito's eyes shone with excitement as she gazed at Poseidon. "I knew you'd take on this task with ease. Come. We have prepared supplies for the journey ahead."

She led Poseidon and Euenor to a cave, its mouth gaping open at the base of the mountain. Strange glyphs and carvings adorned the entrance. Poseidon studied them, but their meaning eluded him.

Cleito lifted a torch and gestured for the men to follow. "Stay close. The tunnels ahead are treacherous."

Poseidon summoned his trident, its glowing prongs casting an ethereal light into the gloom. Together, the trio advanced into the mountain's depths.

The tunnels twisted and turned, sloping ever downward. Poseidon focused on maintaining his footing on the uneven ground. More than once, Euenor threw out an arm to steady him as loose rocks shifted underfoot.

"Have care," he cautioned. "These passages can confuse and mislead."

Poseidon frowned. "Mislead whom?"

"Those who seek the Font's wisdom without wisdom of their own," Euenor replied.

They continued. The air grew heavy and damp, laden with the mineral scent of stone and water.

Cleito halted, holding up a hand. "Wait. Do you hear that?"

Poseidon strained his senses. A faint skittering sound of small feet scraping over stone came from up ahead. He tightened his grip on his trident.

"Ready yourselves," Euenor warned. "We are not alone down here."

Poseidon stepped forward, squinting into the darkness. His trident began to glow brighter, casting light down the tunnel. He perceived shadows shifting on the walls.

"What manner of creatures lurk here?" he asked.

"Cave spiders," Cleito replied. "Their venom is deadly, but they fear the light."

As she spoke, several spiders the size of horses scuttled into view. They cringed away from Poseidon's glowing trident, beady eyes glinting with malice.

Poseidon swept his trident in an arc, driving the spiders back. They hissed and gnashed their fangs. One lunged forward, only to be speared through by the trident's prongs. It let out a shrill death cry.

"We must pass through them to reach the inner sanctum," Euenor said. He drew a long, curved blade from his belt.

Cleito pulled a short sword from her pack. "Stay together. Do not let them surround you."

The trio moved as one, weapons flashing as they cut through the spider horde. Poseidon called on the magic of his trident, unleashing blasts of divine energy that incinerated the spiders by the dozen. But still more poured forth to replace them.

"There are too many!" Cleito cried. She was tired, movements slowing as the spiders pressed their advantage.

Poseidon fought his way to her side. "Take hold of me," he commanded. As soon as her hand clasped his wrist, he summoned the power of the sea. A great wave erupted through the tunnel, washing away the remaining spiders in a churning vortex.

Panting, Poseidon and Cleito found Euenor by a visible stone door at the passage's end.

"Well done," he said. "But ready yourselves. The greatest challenges still lie ahead."

Poseidon and Cleito followed Euenor through the stone door into a vast chamber. Strange machines and advanced technology lined the walls and filled the space.

Cleito's eyes widened. "I've seen nothing like this before. What is all this?"

"Our legacy," Euenor said, touching a metal device. "Knowledge and technology are far beyond anything known to the outside world."

Poseidon examined a wall covered with strange symbols and diagrams. A sense of wonder and possibility stirred within him. The secrets contained here could change everything.

"Do you understand now the importance of what we've found?" Euenor asked.

Cleito nodded. "We cannot let it fall into the wrong hands."

Poseidon met her eyes, seeing his own sense of duty reflected there. Today will be a turning point for them. The hidden legacy of this island had bonded them together.

"We will keep it safe," Poseidon vowed. "You have my word."

Pride shone on Euenor's face. "Then let us begin. Time is short, but there's a lot to learn."

Poseidon felt a thrill of anticipation. Cleito's presence gave him the confidence to face any challenge on their journey. The future stretched before them, bright with possibility.

CHAPTER ELEVEN

The next morning, while mother and daughter went searching for herbs, Poseidon and Euenor embarked on their awe-inspiring journey up the mountain.

Within a half mile of the house, surrounded by pine trees reaching to the sky, was a two-man, silver hovercraft with a blue-and-gold, octagonal star emblem etched onto the side. The craft lifted off the ground with both men aboard.

"What is this?" asked Poseidon, amazed and wide-eyed. "I feel no sensation of movement."

Euenor replied with a knowing smile, "This craft uses anti-gravity technology; it produces no waste emissions and ensures a smooth ride. Let's make a lap around the island!"

The hovercraft sailed over the house. Then Euenor angled the craft toward the summit of the fourteen-thousand-foot snow-capped peak. Tucked into the mountainside was an inner court-yard, aglow with a dazzling, circular agate basin and containing a towering limestone building with exquisite columns.

Euenor opened the Tree of Life—etched glass door by touching an illuminated panel. He and Poseidon stepped inside the holy sanctuary, and a booming voice announced, "Welcome to the Temple of the Pleiades." The star-shaped ceiling above them unfurled like a giant tapestry to reveal a breathtaking view of the morning sky.

The telescope perched at the top shifted in direction through its large, observational opening so that they could view Orion and the Pleiades from within. But this wasn't all; special protection was necessary to preserve such sensitive components of the sophisticated, ground-based telescope. During daylight, Euenor could see puffs of blue clouds passing by, and at night, the stars were right overhead.

The flying craft and sky dome amazed Poseidon. His mind raced with curiosity and excitement as he wondered what Zeus would think about it.

Euenor turned to his visitor with a knowing gleam in his eye. "This sanctuary aligns with the Pleiades star constellation. I am of two worlds: part human from Earth, and part extraterrestrial from the Pleiades. I believe, as a god with special abilities, you can understand the concept of star people."

Poseidon's jaw dropped in awe as he gazed up at the morning sky. He turned to Euenor, searching for an explanation for the gold, eight-angled star on his red jacket. Understanding now flooded his face, and he followed Euenor down a long corridor.

As they neared the end of the hallway, it opened into a laboratory twenty feet high by fifty feet long. It filled its shelves with flasks of all shapes and sizes, lining every wall and reaching up to the ceiling.

A figure appeared at the center of this room, her bluish-silver skin shimmering like quicksilver beneath her white tunic. Silver hair cascaded down her back, and she turned as if expecting their presence.

Euenor introduced Kyrie, a star person from the Pleiades, before beckoning Poseidon closer to hear her explain their planet's strategy.

Kyrie's luminous amber eyes shone with a fierce intensity as her words echoed throughout the lab. "I received a mental transmission late last night, showing that you would arrive today, and I had myself and this laboratory prepared to receive you," she said in a voice steeped in authority.

Poseidon inhaled as he acknowledged the divine presence before him with a reverent bow.

"I come from beyond the stars, from the fifth dimension of light on Taygeta, in the Pleiades star constellation. My form here on Earth is only wearing a humanoid coat of skin. What lies beneath it would be too intimidating for mortal eyes to behold … a ball of energy, an etheric body that exudes a radiant silver-blue hue." She then plucked at her cheek near her mouth, revealing a bright light buried underneath her skin.

Poseidon replied. "I am intrigued by your human form over your energy body. That is amazing."

"Lord Poseidon," she said, her voice melodic yet somber. "I know the pain that gnaws at your spirit."

Poseidon's jaw clenched. His knuckles were white as he gripped his trident. "You know nothing of my torment."

"But I do," Kyrie insisted, drifting closer. "Betrayal by one's own blood is a bitter draught indeed. But you must not let it poison your soul."

Poseidon turned away, staring out at the choppy sea. The waters churned in time with his brewing anger.

"I have not come to heal your wounds, but to reveal your destiny," Kyrie continued. " A great empire called Atlantis will rise from these waters, greater than any built on Mount Olympus. Your legacy."

Poseidon turned back, his stormy gaze meeting her tranquil one. Atlantis? Could this be true? Could he rebuild his power here, in the realm of mortals?

Kyrie stepped forward, placing a delicate hand on his muscular arm. "Help me foster harmony between our peoples, and it will reveal all in time."

Poseidon searched her ancient eyes, so full of wisdom and truth. For the first time since his fall from grace, a flicker of hope rose within him. Here, with the teachings of this celestial prophet, perhaps he could discover his true potential—and build an empire to last eternity.

Poseidon's brows furrowed as he considered Kyrie's words. An empire rising from the seas? The oceans were under his command, yet he never thought of creating something so magnificent.

"Tell me more of this empire," he rumbled. "What is its purpose? Its powers?"

"Allies of like-minded guardians have sent me to your world from Orion with one mission in mind: to find harmony between our two worlds through understanding and knowledge, rather than through violence. This war raging in my time will shape yours if nothing is done, and so I must act to prevent such destruction."

Kyrie's melodic voice grew fervent. "The mysteries of genetics and the Way will fuel Atlantis' new world. Your offspring will gain wondrous abilities—strength, speed, intelligence. But temper these gifts with wisdom and care for the natural world."

Poseidon's pulse quickened. For too long, he had followed Zeus's decrees on Mount Olympus. Now destiny beckoned him down another path, one of discovery and creation.

"I accept your counsel, Kyrie," he declared. "Together we will blaze a new trail for god and mortal alike. But tell me, why have you chosen me for this task?"

Kyrie's eyes crinkled with a smile. "I saw the potential within you, Poseidon. You understand the sea as none other."

Poseidon's chest swelled with purpose. With Kyrie's guidance, he would build an empire from the waves. Harmony with nature and innovation, not conquest. His name would ring out for millennia to come.

Poseidon gazed out at the sea, his mind swirling with Kyrie's revelations. Waves lapped against the rocky shore as he contemplated her words. "A civilization to surpass all others," he murmured. He envisioned grand temples and academies rising from the depths, sanctuaries of learning and culture.

But uncertainty lingered in Poseidon's heart. He turned to Kyrie. "You offer tantalizing a vision, but at what cost? I rule the seas by the grace of Zeus. Will your plans turn us into outcasts?"

Kyrie's expression grew solemn. She placed a hand on his shoulder. "Change always bears a price, but the rewards outweigh the risks. Your subjects will hail you as their visionary leader."

Her voice dropped to a whisper. "Zeus'won't have to be obeyed forever. There are powers he fears, powers we can awaken."

Poseidon's eyes widened. Was she suggesting an open rebellion? Millennia of obedience warred with his yearning for independence.

Kyrie seemed to read his thoughts. "Our path need not be one of conflict. But no longer should you bend your knee when your wisdom equals Zeus's." She squeezed his hand. "The choice is yours, but I am here to guide you."

Poseidon's pulse raced as he turned over her words. She provided knowledge and an opportunity to break free from the past. He would proceed with caution, but his course was clear.

"Then let us begin our work," he declared. With Kyrie's aid, a new era dawned.

Poseidon took a deep breath, steadying himself. Though intrigued by Kyrie's offer, doubts still plagued him. She spoke of power, but power had its price.

He turned to take in the intricate mosaics depicting star charts that adorned the walls and ceilings. Strange devices of unknown origin hummed and blinked on marble pedestals. This was a realm beyond his experience.

"You must have questions," Kyrie said. "This is overwhelming."

Poseidon nodded. "You claim we are kindred souls. But I am a son of Cronus, and ruler of the seas. What do you know of my burdens and duties?"

Kyrie's eyes flashed with empathy. "More than you realize. I, too, carry a great responsibility. My people yearn for a home, and I have vowed to find it."

She gestured to a massive hourglass structure in the temple's center, sand flowing between its two spheres. "That is why I have come. Your realm holds promise for an alliance that will aid us both."

"The enormity of the Federation's choice to make Earth their safe harbor for intergalactic species struck me like a lightning bolt. Even with the Alliance watching over us, I couldn't shake the feeling that perhaps Earth was not yet ready or capable of facing this grand task. Watchers and Mystical Travelers from other galaxies could help us overcome fear, hunger, and survival drives. However, I remained concerned our own conflicts with race and resources would prevent peace throughout the entire Federation."

Poseidon tried to wrap his mind around what he had just heard. Being a god, he could morph a nymph like Cleito's mother, Leucippus, into a mortal. Human hybrids? What was that about? He'd heard Euenor mention he was a human hybrid. "Euenor, explain what you meant by being a human hybrid. How did that happen?"

The regal, silver-haired man's blue eyes sparkled with delight. "My parents were unassuming people who lived in northern Greece. I was told by my mother that one day she had a dream of seeing tall, beautiful ethereal gods. They looked like Kyrie when she has her ethereal coat of skin on."

"The star people took her into a flying craft high in the sky. The gods acted like traditional healers. They did not speak with their mouths, but with their intellects. My mother does not remember what happened to her, except nine months later I was born. People in my family never grew taller than five feet. By fifteen years old, I was seven feet and stronger than my siblings."

"One day when my horse turned lame without knowing why, I put my hands on his leg and began to send him my love. Within minutes, his leg healed. As I matured, I could feel what people were thinking. I developed empathic abilities to see into people."

"As a teenager, I began hearing messages from the star people. I thought I was losing my mind until one day Kyrie appeared in my bedroom. I did not know what to think. She was like a heavenly being sent to me. She clarified why I differed from my siblings. Earth humans are the closest in DNA to the star people of the Pleiades."

"They chose me as the first experiment to change into one of the first hybrid humans. Was it possible for a human to hold the special DNA implanted at the time of my conception? She had been watching for years. At fourteen, Kyrie revealed my identity."

Poseidon nodded. "The DNA. What is that?"

Kyrie answered, walking to the room's heart and waving her right hand to forge a hologram of a long spiral staircase.

Pointing to it, she said, "This is a fragment of DNA. It includes two strands that create a double spiral structure. DNA is the hereditary code in humans, in all organisms, in all galaxies. These elements hold inherited information that allows all forms of life to function, grow, and reproduce. Your height and sea-green eyes are noticeable. There is a language in your blood that gives you these traits. DNA holds the predisposition for more than ninety traits and conditions, ranging from baldness to blindness."

Poseidon's brow knitted as he digested the scientific information. He scratched his head. "Do I understand you are going to use the genetic code inside these bottles to change humans on this planet?"

Kyrie nodded. "Yes. Euenor is an example. He was our first successful human hybrid. Our proposal is to enhance human evolution with star people's DNA. Some DNA gifts will be to strengthen immune systems, grow taller, and expand the use of their creative energy."

"Some extraterrestrials can breathe underwater. Our psyches can communicate over long distances. And we can use our energy to levitate objects. Euenor has these abilities."

Poseidon shook his head. "Can DNA be used for harmful purposes?"

Kyrie and Euenor looked at each other. Euenor replied, "We hope to use the DNA project to help humanity on the planet. What if the bottles get misplaced? The potential damage is unknown."

Poseidon did not know what to think. The gods of the stars planned a massive invasion. He had powers, like lifting weighty objects, throwing lightning, or morphing people and objects. However, introducing a completely new species to this planet? He tried to analyze and understand what the future could be.

Concerned about the impact of the experiment, he stood, hands on his hips, his brow furrowed. "Why did you bring me here? Do you want me to do something?"

Euenor moved forward. He laid his right hand on Poseidon's left arm. Nervous about Poseidon's tone, he cleared his throat. "I can only imagine how crazy this all sounds. Making the planet better through these plans. Yesterday, when you washed up on our shores, I could not believe our luck. We need your help in safeguarding our home and its treasures, as you possess god-like powers. Perhaps with your influence in Greece, you could assist us with bringing people here to our paradise to create our new world. Only with each person's permission will we use new DNA."

"Look at me. I exemplify the new world. The benefits the star people bring are significant. Don't you see?"

CHAPTER TWELVE

Poseidon saw the genuine plea for his help. A sudden shock of awe flooded the god of the sea and horses. Yes, he had special powers, too. His body began to tingle with excitement. Could it be? With a dazed look, he turned to Kyrie with raised enthusiasm.

"Kyrie, if as a god and whose family of Greek gods has special powers, is it possible we are human hybrids and our DNA is from the stars, too? I transformed Cleito's mother from a water nymph into a human woman. Designed the stallion, the bull, mermen, and the Minotaur. And can lift tons of weight and can throw lightning."

The star woman paused and thought about the god's suggestion. She turned to Poseidon. "If you give me permission to take a sample of your saliva, I can assess it to find out where your family's powers might originate. Please sit down in this chair."

Poseidon sat down. His mouth gaped as the star woman took a swap and eased it around the inside of his mouth. Then Kyrie walked to another table and began mixing solutions.

When the test results were ready, the scientist searched her star DNA database for a match. When satisfied with the matchup, Kyrie returned to her guests.

"Yes, Poseidon, you and your god family are human hybrids. Not from the Pleiades, but from Niburu with aliens called the Anunnaki. They came to this planet before us and used DNA to fabricate a superhuman workforce to mine gold from the earth. Your family is the last of their experiment."

"Anunnaki lived for thousands of years in their world. They mined gold on your planet to expand their planet's atmosphere. They left because your planet's one-year short rotation around the sun is 365 days, while their planet Niburu's rotation is fifty years."

Poseidon's mind raced with the origin story of his family. They were a human hybrid experiment for star people as super-human workers. Shocked by the revelation, he turned to Euenor. "At first, when you said you were a human hybrid with special powers, I compared your abilities with mine. We are so different with our special abilities. I am trying to understand the human hybrid concept and what it means to me and you."

He stood wringing his hands. "Throughout my life, I have had to save mortal humans from different monsters who have threatened them, like when I saved Cleito's mother and her sisters from Hades."

Kyrie explained. "The arrival of the Galactic Federation and Mystical Travelers on your planet was a response to the Anunnaki's disregard for the world, resources, and human hy-brids. To correct the negative results of how they used human hybrids, the Federation wanted to bring peace and well-being."

Poseidon listened in shock as the star woman described what the Anunnaki had done. He could believe that they had created two kinds of hybrids: some, like his family, the Greek gods with superhuman abilities, and others meant to be nothing more than slaves. "Marriage to a deity was essential for my family members to pass down their superhuman abilities to their offspring, as marrying a mortal would cause the loss of those powers."

Conflicted, Poseidon stared at the star woman in disbelief. He was unsure how to comprehend the unprecedented information. "Are the Anunnaki still here?"

Kyrie replied, "The Anunnaki left. Greek gods ruled the mortals."

The star woman continued, "We want no differences between slaves and rulers, just people with certain skills but with minor discrepancies among them. Our goal is to produce human hybrids that complement each other without hierarchy. A conscientious mix of individuals who, when propagating, will pass on their successor's helpful characteristics, such as creative minds to direct."

Poseidon stood facing Euenor with his hands open as he spoke. "Kyrie has mentioned Mystical Travelers twice. Who are they? One reason I am here is because of the constant fighting and conflict within the family of gods. I ran away to find peace. Can hybrids flourish without wickedness?"

Euenor listened to the god of the sea. "You are talking about something we are concerned about. We are trying to do something good. What happens if we make things worse in a peaceful environment? Our anxiety stems from the wars of gods. DNA can shape humans to do things."

He paused, making sure Poseidon was following him. "But humans are already likely to dominate their kind. We cannot underestimate the consequences of the changes being made. That is why we summoned Lucas, a Mystical Traveler and Emissary of Light. He will help in the Wisdom School, training in the Code of Love and Light. It will be called The Way for our future kings and people of our nation. You will meet him tomorrow."

Poseidon reflected. He could not believe what he was learning. On this magical island, a plan for a peaceful new beginning might succeed. "Not all the Greek gods are vile. Perhaps with what I have learned within my family, we could develop guidelines for how to work together without fighting among ourselves."

The sea god recognized his compatibility with Kyrie and Euenor's visionary approach to life. He was seeing his future. "Our unity must surpass Greece, even amid divine conflicts. My brother Zeus could be a problem if our home becomes too formidable. We must be mindful of human motivation so that it doesn't undermine the fundamental purpose of peace."

Poseidon stroked his beard. Perhaps they had common ground. And if Kyrie spoke the truth, her knowledge could transform his rule … "Tell me more," he said. "You offer a bold vision. But change bears risks. Convince me this leap is worth taking."

Kyrie nodded, a smile touching her lips. "Then listen and understand."

The genuine work had just begun.

"This is a bold vision," Poseidon said when she had finished. "You offer the power to shape life itself. Knowledge in the wrong hands' spells ruin."

Kyrie answered, "That's why I'm seeking your help." She placed a hand on the hourglass artifact, her eyes distant. "A darkness is coming. There are those who would pervert our gifts for destruction and domination. But united, we can stand against them."

Poseidon's brow furrowed. "Speak. What enemy do you foresee?"

Kyrie turned. Her face etched with sorrow. "The Order of the Black Sun rises in the north—twisted souls obsessed with racial purity. They seek to conquer your lands and enslave your people, using our own arts against us. I hoped to sway them from their ruinous path, but they are beyond reason."

Poseidon tightened his grip on his trident. "Then they shall feel my wrath."

"Another way is possible," Kyrie said. "With wisdom and compassion, we can still light a candle against their darkness. Will you join me on this journey?"

She extended her hand. Poseidon held it after a long look. "For the sake of humanity on land and sea," he spoke. "I pledge myself as your ally."

The hourglass flared, bathing them in a sudden glow. Kyrie spoke, "We have sealed the alliance. We will reveal the consequences of fate as time passes."

Poseidon stood. "Tomorrow I will revisit the ancient temple to discover mysteries. I want to see if I can learn more of my past and the secrets hidden within it."

CHAPTER THIRTEEN

THE ANCIENT TEMPLE LOOMED BEFORE POSEIDON. A CRUMBLING edifice half swallowed by the jungle's greedy embrace. Vines curled around columns, erasing the geometric perfection of their flutes. Stones lay scattered, excavated by roots and the slow creep of entropy. He pressed on, parting leaves with calloused hands. This place predated his reign, but its origins remained shrouded in myth. What secrets lay buried here?

Footsteps echoed down the corridor, too rhythmic for an animal. Poseidon froze, pressing his back against a cool stone. This ancient sanctum did not allow mortals. How had they breached its defenses undetected?

Three figures emerged from the gloom. Black robes flowed around them like living shadows. The leader's face was obscured by a ceramic, demonic mask.

"You trespass in a forbidden realm," the leader intoned. His voice echoed off the walls.

Poseidon stepped into the light. The water in his veins hummed with power. "I walk where I please. Who are you to hinder a god?"

The man stiffened. "One who serves higher powers than you, fallen one."

Rage kindled Poseidon's chest. How dare this mortal claim dominion here? But open confrontation served no purpose. Diplomacy might yield more. "I seek only knowledge, nothing more," he said evenly. "Grant me passage, and no harm will befall you."

The leader's hands slid into his robes. Poseidon tensed. "Our mistress has forbidden your presence here. I cannot defy her will." His hand emerged, clutching an obsidian blade that glowed with dark energy.

Poseidon sighed. So much for diplomacy. He splayed his fingers, and the waters answered. A geyser erupted beneath the men's feet, blasting them backward. Across the floor, the blade of the leader skittered.

Having picked up the dagger for later inspection, the god of the sea walked past their prone bodies. The temple's secrets beckoned. He would allow no one to deny him their revelations.

Poseidon moved deeper into the temple, his footsteps echoing off the stone walls. More robed figures emerged to bar his path, spouting threats and proclamations of forbidden knowledge. He brushed them aside with blasts of water and gusts of wind, their sopping forms left groaning in his wake.

At last, he reached the inner sanctum—a vast circular chamber with a domed ceiling that vanished into darkness. Strange symbols and geometric patterns adorned the walls and floor, illuminated by the aquamarine glow of crystals jutting from the rock. At the chamber's heart sat a stone altar; upon it lay a leather-bound tome and the glint of metal.

Poseidon approached with reverence. This was no ordinary book; he could feel its power thrumming in the air. The metal object was a compass unlike any he'd seen. Its arrows shifted without pattern, reacting to energies beyond the physical realm.

He reached for the leather-bound, worn tome covered in brilliant crystals and secret hieroglyphs, fingers brushing the cover…

"I wouldn't do that if I were you."

Poseidon whirled; the trident leveled. From the shadows stepped Kyrie, hands raised. "Peace, my friend. I will help you. Yesterday, when you announced your return here, I could not allow you to come here alone."

Poseidon lowered his weapon. "How did you find this place?"

She smiled. "I have my ways." Her face grew serious. "Heed my warning; such knowledge comes at a cost. Are you prepared for where this path may lead?"

Poseidon's jaw tightened with resolve. It was too late to turn back. "Take this dagger. I retrieved it from one of the dark acolytes. You might need it."

Kyrie laughed. "Okay, but I have ways you have not seen to defend us both."

Poseidon yanked the tome out from its sheath, and a powerful jolt of electricity surged through his veins. Visions flooded his mind - of the past and future prophecies. The realization hit him like a lightning bolt: this was an Anunnaki temple for gods to open. Was a network of these temples possible?

In an instant, thousands of images swept through his mind's eye—the ancient overseers, the Anunnaki; his ancestors, Uranus, and his entourage of human-hybrid slaves; then his father, Cronus, wresting power from Uranus; he and his siblings being cast into Tartarus by their own father; and the Olympians' war upon the Titans. Further still, he saw flashes of the future. Himself and Cleito, together with Lucas, the Mystical Traveler, laying foundations for a peaceful new world. But beyond that, the vision faded into obscurity.

The compass needles spun before settling into alignment. The path forward was now clear.

Poseidon's mind reeled as the visions faded. So many revelations in mere moments—his own origins, the true nature of Atlantis, the Order of the Black Sun's insidious plans. It would take time to process everything.

He turned to Kyrie. "You knew this would happen. Why didn't you stop me?"

She tilted her head. "Who am I to obstruct a god's search for answers? This is your journey to walk, no matter where it leads."

Poseidon nodded, grateful for her wisdom. Together, they studied the aligned compass, speaking in hushed tones about all they had witnessed. Though shaken, Poseidon felt emboldened by the knowledge he now held. To face the future, he needed his allies' support and counsel. "The Order seeks to pervert the power of Atlantis," he said. "We cannot let that happen."

Kyrie clasped his shoulder. "Then we won't. But remember power corrupts even the best intentions. Guard yourself against pride."

"I will. With you at my side."

She smiled. "Always."

Poseidon raised his trident, feeling its power thrum through him. "Onward. We have work to do."

The compass needles held steady, guiding them into destiny's unfolding mystery.

Poseidon and Kyrie ventured deeper into the ancient ruins, following the direction shown by the mystical compass. The crumbling walls and columns surrounded them on all sides as they descended through echoing chambers and vast halls.

Poseidon's senses were on high alert, probing the shadows for any sign of danger. His grip on the trident tightened. The artifact's revelations meant the Order was close by.

Rounding a corner, he froze. Strange symbols and geometric shapes glowed along the walls, pulsing with an eldritch light. Poseidon's eyes widened. This was no ordinary site; the entire room thrummed with arcane energy.

"A ritual chamber," Kyrie murmured. She traced her fingers over the glyphs, brow furrowed. "Used for powerful magic. But what were they conjuring here?"

Poseidon joined her and observed the place. A bitter sense of foreboding crept through him. The compass trembled.

"The ritual … it's not over."

At that moment, the glyphs flared brighter. The chamber rumbled, dust cascading from the ceiling. From the shadows emerged three figures in dark robes, eyes blazing crimson.

Poseidon brandished his trident. This must be the Order leaders' gathering place.

Kyrie drew the black obsidian blade Poseidon had given her. Figures draped in hooded black robes stalked closer, ancient magic crackling at their fingertips. Poseidon's muscles tensed.

The battle was on.

Poseidon's grip on his trident tightened as the robed figures approached. He could feel the power radiating from them— ancient, arcane, and deadly. These were no mere acolytes but masters of the occult arts.

With a guttural chant, the lead figure extended its hands. Crimson lightning arced from its fingertips toward Poseidon.

He deflected it with a sweep of his trident; the bolt exploding against a column in a shower of stone shards. "You will not pass," he bellowed, his voice booming through the chamber. "Atlantis holds secrets not meant for you."

The figure hissed in response, foul magic warping its voice. "Atlantis will be ours. The new era is at hand."

It unleashed another volley of eldritch lightning. Poseidon summoned a wall of water to absorb the blast. Steam erupted in clouds as mystic energies sizzled against the barrier.

On the flank, Kyrie darted forward, her obsidian knife-edge slashing back with evil powers in a silvery blur. She severed the casting hand of one acolyte in a spray of blood. It howled, stumbling back.

The lead figure gestured with an invisible force toward Kyrie. With a leap, the star woman crashed into her attacker. He fell into a pillar and slid down, stunned.

Rage boiled within Poseidon. The sea mirrored his fury. The ground rumbled as the waters surrounding Atlantis churned and swelled.

Robed figures paused, exchanging glances. Poseidon leveled his trident, eyes blazing. "You will go no farther. Atlantis holds its secrets still."

A rumble grew into a roar as a massive wave surged through the chamber entrance. At Poseidon's command, it smashed the masters aside and receded, leaving only silence and receding water behind.

Poseidon exhaled, lowering his trident.

He strode through the now empty chamber, his footsteps echoing off the ornate walls. Mosaics and carvings depicted the

Anunnaki, fantastical sea creatures and scenes from Atlantis's storied past. He paused before a faded image of himself from eons ago, strong and proud.

How far he had fallen since those glory days. Cast out by Zeus, stripped of his power and domain. Atlantis was all he had left now. This island and its secrets were his last link to who he once was.

Poseidon ran his hand over the mosaic, brow furrowed. There in the hidden depths, he could feel them calling to him, tantalizing whispers from the distant past.

With renewed determination, he delved deeper into the ancient passages. Glowing crystals lit the way as he descended crumbling stairs into realms untouched for millennia. The air grew heavy with power the farther he ventured.

Strange writings covered the walls, languages lost to time. Poseidon murmured the words to himself, snippets of meaning coming back to him. References to bloodlines, ancient rites, gates long sealed.

A vast archway loomed before him, inscribed with intricate runes. Poseidon could sense the hidden messages woven into it, warning any with ill intent to turn back. He placed his hand upon it, channeling his power.

The barrier shuddered as it dissolved, and a gaping maw of darkness opened before him. With a deep breath, he imagined an orb of light within his fist and stepped inside.

Driven to find answers about his identity and potential, he moved onward as the past called to him. Without hesitation, he marched toward his destiny.

To decipher a rune on the wall, he dropped his lighted orb in a crash that echoed through the chamber. When he stooped to pick it up, he noticed an eerie sigil chiseled onto the stone floor—a black sun surrounded by a sinister pentagram.

"Kyrie, look at this," Poseidon breathed and stepped nearer for a closer inspection.

Kyrie nodded. "It's a symbol of the Order of the Black Sun."

They crossed the dark symbol and found an oak door with an engraved Black Sun symbol.

Kyrie spoke in hushed tones. "Yes, I sense something beyond this door. Let me cast my spell of invisibility, and we can gain entry without being seen or heard."

Poseidon gaped in surprise at Kyrie's suggestion. "You can make us invisible?"

Kyrie chuckled softly and gave him an encouraging smile. "I told you I could help keep us safe."

The angel of light stood there, her luminescent body a soft golden glow in the cavern. At first, Poseidon saw only the shape of her nude form and the faint outline of her legs. Then he blinked his eyes to bring them into focus, and she was standing before him, radiant with light. He could feel its warmth spreading through him as she spoke.

Her voice sparkled. "Can you see my glowing form?" She glowed brighter as she asked.

Poseidon gasped at the transformation. "Yes. Now what?"

She replied. "Okay, close your eyes and imagine you and I are one. Imagine it's just you and me in this cave."

Poseidon closed his eyes and began to feel himself enveloped in her brilliant light. "Oh, I feel your light," he whispered.

Kyrie announced, "I'm creating a veil of invisibility." She turned off her light and covered herself with the invisibility shield. The fabric of the shield swallowed her light as it protected her from view while allowing her to breathe.

Poseidon reached out and placed his trident against the door, half expecting to feel pain or unseen hands grabbing at him, but nothing happened. He pushed his body against the oak wood door and frowned when he realized it would not allow him to pass through it.

Kyrie laughed quietly beside him and grabbed his arm. "Don't worry. Come on." She pulled the god toward her and ran through the oak wood door in front of him. He followed behind.

CHAPTER FOURTEEN

Down the path, Poseidon saw the cavernous chamber reverberated with the discordant humming of the Black Sun. In its center, the seven-foot Artemis stood tall and defiant in her knee-length tunic, her golden tresses bound tightly around her head like a halo of power. She was "the goddess of three forms"—Selene in the sky, Artemis on earth, Hecate in the underworld and above. As Hecate, she held dominion over darkness, wielding deeds of insidious, malevolent magic, a force that could transform creatures by manipulating their DNA. Her project, the Black Sun, was an act of rebellion against her twin brother, Apollo—a plan to usurp his position as God of the Sun and bring the ancient Vril up from within the Earth's womb.

The night was pitch black. A new moon eclipse rose in Scorpio, the ruler of black magic. Back at the shrine, Artemis called the five priests into her service.

Draped in a voluminous leopard-skin cloak, Artemis exuded an aura of power as she spoke. The five secretive servants in black obeyed her command and placed their ominous, ruby-studded walking sticks into the pattern of the Black Sun on the floor. As the lightning bolt began to rise, Hecate's presence almost seemed to electrify the air. Her voice resonated throughout the chamber like thunder.

Poseidon felt strange. Even cloaked, he could feel a pulsing energy. He heard a soft hum. He wrinkled his brow and whispered to Kyrie, "When I entered the room, it felt like a force flowed over me."

Artemis smiled. "Welcome to our inaugural assembly of the Society of Truth; you are about to witness something unprecedented. I will grant those who join us unrivaled power."

Artemis moved closer, her heart racing as the five priests of darkness bowed in reverence. "Behold the power of the ruby crystal! Its magnificent source can elevate our minds and magnify our abilities!"

The pentagram lit up like lightning bolts from beneath the feet of the Black Sun and their initiates, forming a shimmering stage that seemed to hum with an ancient energy. The dark priests raised their golden staffs, each one topped by a ruby gemstone, drawing out still more energy from within the depths. A deafening roar filled the temple as the ritual began.

All who gathered reached a silent agreement. "It is time," Artemis declared in a powerful voice. "Raise your golden rods and feel the power of the Vril coursing through you and charging your lightning rods!" Flames burst from each walking staff as the crowd erupted into loud cheers.

Then came the Lord of Chaos, Apep, an ancient demon giant snake with six legs crawling out of the pentagram and wrapping itself around Artemis's stave like a pet. This eater of souls lived in the underworld and lurked beneath the realm of sunrise or sunset, ready to attack those foolish enough to anger it.

The five priests who attended this Black Sun ceremony felt an evil presence that shook them to their core. They had dedicated themselves to experiments on the DNA of humans and other animals, but now they knew what true power lay within the depths of the Black Sun.

A wave of anticipation rippled through the crowd as Artemis, the High Priestess of Darkness, stepped forward. Gleaming like a star in the night sky, she held her hands aloft to reveal five priests of darkness standing at the altar.

"My children," she began with a voice that was both powerful and soothing. "I have chosen these five to lead you on our journey to greatness. Together, we will break free from our mortal bonds and ascend into immortality!"

The crowd erupted in cheers as Artemis's electric energy crackled between her fingertips.

"We will become like gods—invincible and all-powerful! The future is ours for the taking!"

The assembled faithful couldn't contain their excitement. With Artemis leading them onward, they had a bright and glorious destiny ahead.

"But only the worthy will join our ranks," she continued. "We are the elite, the chosen. Our blood purified, our bodies enhanced. We'll dominate all worlds."

Thunder rumbled overhead, as if in approval. Artemis raised her arms. "I chose you for your unwavering allegiance to me! Poseidon and his minions would have us on our knees, but we will never bow in servitude!"

The crowd erupted with an avalanche of cheers. "Long live Hecate!"

A sly smirk tugged at the corners of Artemis's lips. Her devoted followers were ready and willing to fulfill her desire: to demolish the outdated power structure and raise a new era under her command.

"This is only the beginning." In the swirl of her leopard-skin cloak, the proud goddess marched out of the ceremonial chamber in retreat to her science lab.

Poseidon and Kyrie watched from inside their cloak of invisibility as Artemis rallied her followers. Poseidon clenched his trident, his anger simmering. How dare she threaten him? Him, the great earthshaker, ruler of the seas! He should drown her precious cult now—send waves to swallow them all.

But no. He must be cautious. Artemis had grown unpredictable. He needed to know more about this "Dark Sun." What were her true aims? This talk of transcendence and blood purification disquieted him.

As the crowd dispersed, Artemis retreated to a chamber down the cavern passageway. Poseidon watched, merging into mist. Once inside, his eyes widened.

Still cloaked, he and Kyrie followed the dark mistress. In the open stone room, strange machinery hummed, illuminated by arcane glyphs. Cages held creatures that seemed to shift between human and beast in agonized shapes. Artemis stood over a medical slab, inspecting a writhing satyr strapped upon it.

"Begin the infusion," she commanded. Her followers inserted needles into the satyr, pumping vials of shimmering blue liquid into its veins. It thrashed before going still, chest rising with slow breaths.

Poseidon had seen enough. He slipped away, mind racing. This cult was dangerous, their experiments an affront to nature itself. But Artemis was no fool. Her powers had grown … as had her madness.

He would need allies. Before him, twisted visions plunged the world into chaos. The seas still bowed to him.

Time to remind the mortals of the darkness.

CHAPTER FIFTEEN

Poseidon emerged with Kyrie from the hidden chamber, his immortal heart heavy with concern. Artemis's descent into madness was worse than he had feared. Her cult's dark experiments posed a grave threat that he could not face alone.

Kyrie said, "I am going to remove our cloaking device."

They returned to their mortal forms.

As he and Kyrie strode through the empty halls, the soft click of footsteps made him pause. He turned and saw a young woman approaching. She wore a black robe etched with arcane symbols, marking her as a member of the Order. Dark hair cascaded over her shoulders, and intelligent eyes assessed him.

"Lord Poseidon," she greeted with a respectful bow. "We did not expect you to honor us with your presence."

Despite himself, her composure impressed him. She showed no fear of being near a god. "I wished to look upon my niece's work," he replied.

The woman's gaze was piercing. "And what do you think of it?"

Poseidon chose his next words carefully. "This cultist was no mindless follower. Artemis has been alone for a while. Her work is demonic."

The woman nodded. "Lady Artemis's visions are not ours to judge. We follow where she leads, without question." Her tone made it clear any attempt to sway her loyalty would fail.

"Loyalty is an admirable quality," Poseidon said. "But blind obedience carries its own risks."

Despite her defiant eyes, the woman bowed her head. "My name is Madeline," she proclaimed, tossing her chestnut hair over her shoulder and gracing Poseidon with a triumphant smile.

Poseidon returned the gaze of her deep, sea-green eyes and said, "What do you want?"

Madeline smirked knowingly. "Come with me to where the five priests of the Dark Sun are gathering. You will witness the true power shown through our rituals. Initiates like me are privy to what lies within—a strength so great it brings terror to all who dare cross it. Join me in accessing this unfathomable force, Poseidon. Mind your step or face your doom."

Poseidon watched her, determined yet cautious. Artemis had chosen fanatics who were hard to destroy. A spark of hope lingered in the shadows, one that begged for someone to act against the evil that was taking hold. He steeled himself and declared, "Kyrie, let us join Madeline and enter the chamber of darkness at the Black Sun altar."

In the torch-lit chamber of the Dark Sun, the five high-ranking, robed priests with their lightning rods knelt before a towering obsidian idol. The air hummed with energy as they chanted in unison, their voices rising and falling in hypnotic cadence.

At the idol's feet lay offerings of gold, jewels, and vials of blood. The cultists swayed, consumed by religious ecstasy. All thoughts bent toward a single purpose—pleasing their dark mistress.

Unseen, Poseidon observed. This ritual channeled power to Artemis to strengthen her connection to ancient forces.

The chanting reached fever pitch, then halted. A tall, broad-shouldered man stood, turning to face the silent cultists. "Brothers. Sisters," he intoned. "The time of purification is nigh. Our lady calls, and we shall answer."

Murmured prayers of obedience answered him. With a gesture, two robed figures came forward, dragging a bound and hooded prisoner between them.

The prisoner struggled as they forced him before the idol and ripped away his hood. A young man huddled, pale and trembling. The leading cultist approached, drawing a curved ceremonial blade.

He proclaimed, "Your blood and bone shall sanctify our race," while raising the blade high with arcs of black energy dancing along its edge.

The prisoner whimpered in terror.

Poseidon had seen enough. He emerged from the shadows, his trident materializing in his grip. "This sacrilege ends now!" His voice boomed through the chamber like thunder.

The cultists turned, shock and outrage twisting their faces. Poseidon braced for battle. Blood would flow this night.

But not his.

The leading cultist hissed, lowering his blade. "You dare interfere with our blessed rites, sea god?"

Poseidon leveled his trident, the prongs beginning to glow with azure light. "Your rites are an abomination. Release the boy."

The cultist's lip curled in a sneer. With a flick of his wrist, he drew a line across the prisoner's throat. Dark arterial blood sprayed forth as the young man crumpled.

"No!" Poseidon shouted in dismay. But it was too late.

The cultist cast the bloody blade aside. "His sacrifice strengthens our cause. As will yours."

He raised his hands, malignant energy rippling. Following their lead, the other cultists created arcs of black lightning between their ruby staves. Poseidon felt his hair stand on end as the air crackled with power.

Hatred filled the eyes of the lead cultist. "You cannot stop the coming storm, sea god."

Poseidon pointed his trident at the man's heart. "I can stop you."

He hesitated. Slaying these misguided mortals would only martyr them. He must find another way.

The cultist seethed with rage, his desperate plea a veiled threat. "You are nothing. Dare you challenge our ambition? Join us and we will make you all-powerful!"

Poseidon's gaze flamed like molten steel, unflinching in the face of fear as he spat out an icy reply. "Never!"

Cursing, the five dark priest cultists lunged forward, their electrified staves crackling with malicious power. In a flash, Poseidon swung his trident up in an arc, deflecting the energy back onto them.

Fueled by an inner fire and righteous fury, Poseidon swept the staff across the room like wildfire, decimating everything in its path, including the Dark Sun pentagram on the floor. It silenced the screams of the priests in the chamber.

Poseidon faced Madeline and the remaining cultists with a menacing stare. He warned, "You must choose your path, because this one only leads to ruin."

Madeline, a high initiate, watched Poseidon destroy the five high priests alongside the Black Sun temple that had been her home for so long. The event shook her faith in Artemis and the Order of the Black Sun.

Madeline searched for an answer among her acolyte friends, who had also seen Poseidon destroy their temple. "Do you doubt Artemis and our beliefs?"

The three companions, each battling their own thoughts, looked startled and confused.

Then he and Kyrie left the dark cave, leaving the cultists to ponder his words.

CHAPTER SIXTEEN

A TRIUMPHANT ARTEMIS STRODE THROUGH THE DOORS OF THE Black Sun temple, her movements flowing with a newfound energy. Her proud blue eyes were ablaze, and success radiated from her beautiful face. Silver robes whipped around her as cultists scampered away in fear.

She barreled into the laboratory like an enraged tempest, scattering everyone out of her path. Her lead geneticist shrank back at his workstation, quivering in terror. "Why do you cower? You should be ecstatic with the surge of new acolytes," she snarls.

"My lady, progress is being made, but the mutations remain unstable. We will need more test subjects before we perfect the process," he stammered.

Artemis exploded in rage and seized him by the throat with ironclad strength. She spit her condemnation right onto his face—"Then find more subjects!"—before flinging him against the wall like a rag doll.

She turned to a figure strapped to a metal table, IV tubes running into his arms. He was a hybrid of man and beast, muscles rippling under coarse fur. His lips peeled back, revealing fangs that could tear a man apart.

Artemis ran a hand along his arm. "A valiant effort, but still flawed. We must keep trying."

She whirled to face her scientists. "Resume your work. The next iteration will serve my purposes, or you will suffer the same fate as your failed experiments."

They scrambled to obey as Artemis swept from the room. She had come too far to be thwarted now. The power of a god was within her grasp. Failure was not an option.

She descended to the deepest chamber, the domain of her most promising subject. A human woman floated in a vat of viscous fluid, tubes invading her flesh. Artemis placed a hand on the glass.

"Soon, my child," she crooned. "You'll be the first member of a new race. The dawn of my empire."

Her form flickered, the glamor falling away to reveal a face marred by hatred and ambition. Artemis the huntress was gone. Only Hecate remained.

She strode through the stone corridors of the temple, torchlight flickering across her stern features, and entered the ritual chamber, where robed figures stood around a stone altar. Upon it lay a man, stripped naked, terror in his eyes. Artemis approached and placed a ceremonial dagger against his chest.

"You have the honor of serving our noble purpose," she intoned. "Sacrifice brings power."

The man whimpered pleas for mercy. Artemis silenced him with a look. She drew the blade across his throat in one swift motion. Blood spilled across the altar.

The disciples chanted arcane words as Artemis lifted her arms, reveling in the offering. She could feel the energy coursing through her. She was one step closer to her goal.

Footsteps echoed down the corridor. A disciple appeared breathless. "My lady, Poseidon has destroyed the Black Sun chamber and the priests. We must flee."

Rage twisted Artemis's face. Poseidon would pay for his interference. But now was not the time. "Gather our work," she commanded. "We will find a new temple."

She swept from the chamber, disciples rushing to erase all traces of their presence. Poseidon might slow her progress, but he could not stop destiny. The new race would rise. Failure was not an option.

Artemis swept through the stone corridors, her disciples scrambling around her to gather their research and resources.

"Hurry!" she commanded. "Leave nothing behind!"

How dare Poseidon interfere! Her life's work was too important to be stopped by that arrogant fool.

CHAPTER SEVENTEEN

THE NEXT DAY, BIRDS OF THE ENCHANTED JUNGLE SANG AS Poseidon watched Euenor and Kyrie in reverent prayer. Each sat in the garden between two twenty-foot obelisks adorned with sacred symbols, chanting the name of the universal god, HU, as the early-morning broke in bright reds and golds across the brilliant blue sky.

Then the air went silent. The flora and fauna listened to the wind of creation. The air smelled sweet with purple and white jasmine. A loving wash of euphoria came over Poseidon as the energy of their transcendent chanting spiraled around him.

Kyrie's blue-silver skin radiated bright light; her eyes were closed, her hands incandescent in prayer. "In loving, we call forward the Mystical Traveler Lucas from the sixth dimension of light to connect with us in his physical body."

A radiant and gentle man, adorned in an indigo floor-length tunic cinched with a golden sash, emerged between the obelisks, bathed in a swirl of golden-violet light in the shape of infinity, from the spiritual sky of the universe, accompanied by the tinkling sound of bells.

Poseidon stared at the bringer of light materializing from the sixth dimension to the third. Overwhelmed by the spectacle, tears streamed down his face. The god of the sea's heart opened as the loving from Lucas swept over him. A calm happiness spilled over inside as the gaze of God's joy elated him.

Little by little, the teacher materialized. First, the heavenly illumination slipped down to show his noble face. His dark-brown eyes held a radiance of compassion and understanding. A corona of light circled his light-brown, shoulder-length hair. With his limbs resting at his sides, Lucas stood in simple majesty. The two mighty men complemented each other.

The god of the sea stood motionless, mesmerized by Lucas. A wave of serenity rolled off the man like sunshine after a storm. Poseidon felt humbled in the presence of someone so saintly.

The bringer of light shone as he stood, exuding radiant love.

Euenor motioned for Poseidon and Lucas to follow him to the pagoda near the house. When they arrived, Cleito had jasmine tea and fresh biscuits waiting for them.

They sat on bamboo chairs around a circular oak table. The enigmatic person caught Poseidon's curiosity as they passed around food and tea. "I have a family of gods; do you?"

Lucas set his teacup down and smiled. "I am one of many Mystical Travelers who will come to this planet throughout history to help humans move forward in a positive direction. Some of us Travelers will start as humans who received the mystical connection to the sixth realm of light."

Poseidon reflected. "What is the sixth realm of light?"

Lucas explained, "Mystical Travelers in the sixth-dimension travel through time in an energy form. The sixth dimension is that of light, faith, purity. Travelers bring the Creator's light energy to Earth from that dimension. Many will introduce new ways of thinking and provide spiritual guidance."

Poseidon speculated on how potent the Creator could be. After all, he could throw lightning. Wasn't that power?

Lucas tuned into Poseidon's brainwaves and smiled. "Oh, so you are seeing yourself throwing lightning and wondering how much mightier the Creator could be?"

Poseidon's eyes widened with surprise. *What? Can he read my mind?*

Lucas laughed. "Be cautious with an open mind. Through my compassion, I am sensitive to people's feelings. I tune into people and understand their experiences."

Poseidon shook his head. *Read other people's minds? I can barely keep up with my own thoughts.* "Who, or what, is the Creator?"

Lucas replied, "The Creator is ineffable, inspired love. A loving being of light desires peace for all, like a parent seeing their child for the first time. The love of the Creator for us is greater than that experience."

Poseidon wanted to know more. "Will the Mystical Travelers always be successful when they call on our planet with their wisdom teachings?"

Lucas responded, "No, not always. Travelers stay here to aid human consciousness. We tried working with the Anunnaki, but their agenda of taking the planet's resources did not fit within our principles of peace. Our proposal requires people's choice. People have lifestyle choices. Our purpose is peace, not war."

The teacher sipped his tea and continued, "This planet is one of change. In a challenging experiment, we hope to innovate a movement called The Way. From living in dread of change to living in love through one's spiritual heart. It may sound easy, but the human condition resists change. The Way teaches people how to manage change, chaos, and worry. To live with ease and grace. Hopefully, with the help of Kyrie and the human hybrid experiment, people will live with open hearts and minds."

Lucas gazed at Kyrie, who looked worried. "What bothers you, star child?"

Kyrie's voice trembled as she placed a hand on the hourglass artifact. "A darkness is here," she warned, her eyes distant. "The Order of the Black Sun rises in the north, their goal nothing less than our total defeat and domination. They have embraced our powers, twisting them to serve their own ends and wicked desires."

Poseidon nodded in agreement. "I have encountered some of them and their dark arts. They mean to destroy the good of Atlantis and instill their dark practices."

Kyrie turned away, her face etched with sorrow. "I had hoped to sway them from their ruinous path, but it seems they are too far gone. I fear we face a level of conflict that is likely to become deadly. Is there anything you can do, Lucas, in our battle of darkness versus light?"

Lucas's eyes glinted with an otherworldly illumination as he stood up, his voice reverberating through the chamber. "I possess a power beyond time itself," he declared, drawing out a small lead box from his pocket. "The Shamir Stone can create and destroy at my command. I suggest we build sacred temples across this land—structures reinforced by the holy light of the heavens, impervious to darkness and chaos."

Poseidon's eyes burned with intensity as he surveyed Euenor and Kyrie, his voice reverberating through the air like thunder. "Then we shall forge the blessed isle of Atlantis," he proclaimed.

Lucas nodded in approval. "That is what should be done. The Mystical Travelers believe you are the right one to lead Atlantis. And I believe the heart of the isle must have a temple of Atlantis. Will you accept guiding Atlantis natives to a future governed by The Way, despite the dangers?"

Poseidon's mind raced as he contemplated the ramifications of his decision. Steeling himself, he spoke with resolve. "Yes. I am humbled by this choice. I look forward to constructing a temple for all conscientious citizens to learn The Way."

The three raised their cups in unison, voices echoing off the walls. "To sacred Atlantis and Poseidon's Temple. May Atlanteans find The Way!"

CHAPTER EIGHTEEN

Poseidon stood at the edge of a craggy cliff, his trident glinting in the sunlight as he gazed out over the vast expanse of churning ocean. The sea breeze ruffled his hair and beard as he contemplated the task before him. It was time to end Artemis's reign of terror upon them.

He turned as Lucas and Kyrie approached. Lucas wore a leather tool belt laden with instruments for his craft. Kyrie's cloak billowed around her in the wind, her amber eyes glinting with arcane power.

"The site is ideal," Lucas said, gesturing to the cliffs. "We can construct supports into the rock to form a foundation."

Poseidon nodded. "Begin at once. We must work quickly if we are to complete the Temple of Poseidon before Artemis catches wind of our plans."

He tightened his grip on the trident, turning to watch Lucas scratching notes into a leather journal, brow furrowed in concentration. Poseidon allowed himself a small smile. Artemis would not expect him to recruit the help of immortals. That would prove to be her downfall.

The sun climbed higher as they set to work.

"Let's review the plans," Poseidon said, unrolling a large scroll across the sand. "The walls here and here require reinforcement." He pointed along the perimeter of the temple blueprint.

Lucas retrieved the lead box from his pocket. "The Shamir is one of ten mysterious artifacts created by God at twilight on the sixth day of creation. It is a supernatural worm the size of a single grain of barleycorn. Its gaze is so powerful that it can cut through any material with ease, even though diamond itself, the hardest substance on Earth."

Kyrie asked, "Why is the Shamir called a stone when it's a worm?"

Lucas replied, "The Shamir is called a stone to keep its identity secret. Recognizing a Shamir as a worm requires prior knowledge. And the tiny lead box in which it rests looks like a stone."

"A lead container holds the Shamir, wrapped in wool, while it rests and travels the inner realms of light until we need it in the Earth realm. Any other vessel would melt and disintegrate under the Shamir's gaze."

Poseidon stood with his golden trident. He swept the sky with a bolt of lightning. His staff charged with electrical current. With the Shamir's laser, Lucas dug into the earth using his staff. Lucas stood next to Poseidon, chanting sacred tones of light and energy. The two moved together like a dance. Energy of light and sound from Lucas energized Shamir to cut deep into the earth.

Shamir's intense shaft of light traveled through the air, slicing with precision the three rings of earth and water, connecting them via a canal to the outer perimeter of the main landmass. As the Shamir elevated the landscape, Andara crystals tumbled out of the soil, dotting the landscape with monatomic energy, joining the angelic spirits of the dolphins, whales, and other oceanic beings of light with great love to protect with the light within all beings.

Poseidon ensured that the concentric zones of land and water were perfect, creating two earth and three water zones around the key island and providing irrigation through two springs.

When the mystical talisman finished designing the three new rings of topography and water, the Shamir's laser, together with Lucas's supernatural brain power and Poseidon's inner light, transported the landscape two miles out into the deep sea, where an unnamed island formed.

Lucas traced his finger across the page. "I will put the Shamir onto the drawings to reinforce those areas with thicker blocks of granite. It can withstand even a giant's blow." He set the Shamir over the construction plans. It hovered, absorbing the images.

Poseidon rolled up the scroll, satisfied. "Then let's begin."

Shamir's gaze released a beam of light that hit the stone. In moments, the light cut the rocks to the measurements of the drawing it had absorbed.

After cutting all the massive stones, Lucas asked for Kyrie's help. With focused concentration, they raised their hands and projected powerful energy that reversed gravity and polarity. As if weightless, the multi-ton stones rose and moved into place.

By late afternoon, the outer walls stood towering and impenetrable. Inside, the temple's central chamber was taking shape, flanked by pillars etched with ancient symbols of power.

Poseidon wiped sweat from his brow, pride swelling in his chest. This monument would stand for millennia, a testament to his reign. Neither god nor titan would threaten his domain again.

Kyrie assisted with her magic, levitating the largest stones into place. Poseidon called forth the powers of the sea, commanding the waves to bring sand and clay to form the temple's mortar.

By sunset, the basic structure was in place. With silver and gold foils on limestone and golden statuary surrounding it, the sacred Temple of Poseidon rose to a height of ninety-eight feet.

The contrast of elements was in keeping with the esoteric principle of honoring opposites. The spiritual equilibrium—in this case, gold representing the sun and silver representing the moon—represented the ultimate expressions of male and female energies: solar being male and lunar, female.

Through the glass doors, inside the place of worship, stood a thirty-foot-high atrium. At the focal point of the sanctuary stood a solid orichalcum pillar on which The Shamir had engraved the laws of Atlantis.

Poseidon rested his hand on a column. Soon, his niece would learn that none could challenge his domain. His reign over the seas would remain absolute.

The Temple of Poseidon would stand as an eternal reminder of that truth.

Lucas ran a handkerchief over his forehead, shielding his eyes from the sun as he glanced at the towering stone walls of the temple. Picking up his worn leather book and the box containing the precious Shamir, he stumbled back to his tent, where a single lantern illuminated the makeshift workbench inside.

Kyrie floated down from where she had been levitating stones into place. "I set the wards. No sorcery will breach these walls."

Poseidon nodded, satisfied. Though incomplete, the temple already radiated power—a monument to the new Atlantis and The Way.

"We should rest," Lucas suggested. "Tomorrow will bring more challenges."

As the sun sank below the horizon, they retreated to tents on the beach. Kyrie hummed softly, conjuring a campfire with a flick of her wrist. Flames crackled, casting a warm glow over their makeshift encampment.

Despite his exhaustion, Poseidon found sleep elusive. Trident in hand, he gazed into the darkness from the water's edge. Artemis was out there somewhere, plotting her next move. He would need to be ready.

The steady sound of waves lapping the shore calmed his restless mind. He allowed himself a small smile. Soon Artemis would regret ever defying him.

When morning came, they would continue their work. Stone by stone, the temple would rise. It would secure Poseidon's dominance.

CHAPTER NINETEEN

POSEIDON AWOKE BEFORE DAWN, ENERGIZED TO CONTINUE work on the temple. As he stepped outside, a prickle of unease crept down his spine. An unnatural stillness hung over the site. The morning sky was dark, with no hint of the coming sunrise.

Poseidon tightened his grip on his trident as he scanned the area. Where were the workers? They should have arrived by now.

A rasping voice echoed from the shadows. "Dear uncle, did you think your pathetic construction would go unnoticed?"

Artemis emerged, flanked by hulking beasts with the heads of bulls and the bodies of men. Behind them slithered a hoard of snakelike monsters, hissing and baring fangs.

Poseidon's eyes blazed with fury. "You will meet your defeat, Artemis."

She cackled. "No, I will meet your end."

With blinding speed, she drew back her bow and loosed an arrow aimed at Poseidon's heart. He deflected it with his trident and charged, bellowing a war cry.

The Minotaur lumbered forward to intercept him. Poseidon ducked under a sweeping axe and drove his trident up through one of the creatures' ribs. It collapsed, but more closed in. The snake monsters encircled him, spitting venom.

Poseidon fought on, the trident spinning and thrusting. But Artemis stayed back, nocking arrows, and picking off doves in the trees.

Soon Poseidon was tiring. The Minotaur' axes found their mark, leaving gashes across his arms and chest. The snakes' toxic bites seared his skin.

Artemis smiled coldly, savoring his pain. "You should have stayed in your watery realm, Poseidon. The land is mine to rule."

She drew back an arrow for the killing shot. Poseidon roared in defiance and charged again, even as darkness crept into his vision ...

A blast of magical energy incinerated the snakes closest to him. Kyrie descended from the sky, eyes glowing white-hot, hands wreathed in crackling flames.

With a sweep of her arm, she immolated a swath of Minotaur. Poseidon regained his footing, reinvigorated.

Artemis scowled. "Meddlesome witch!" She redirected her bow, but Kyrie erected a shimmering barrier to deflect the arrows.

"We won't let you win, Artemis," Kyrie declared.

Behind the Minotaur, metal jaws sprang from the earth, snapping shut around legs and hooves. Lucas had activated his Shamir traps. The Minotaur bellowed as the mechanisms crushed or impaled them.

Artemis shrieked in frustration. "You fools delay the inevitable!"

"No," said Poseidon, hefting his trident. "Your reign of terror ends now."

The three advanced in unison—Poseidon radiating divine fury, Kyrie wreathed in mage fire, Lucas coolly preparing more mystical traps. Artemis retreated. She shape-shifted into a red hawk and flew into the dark forest.

Poseidon started to chase, but Kyrie stopped him. "Let her go. We've won this battle."

Lucas clapped Poseidon on the shoulder. "The temple still stands. And we stand together."

Poseidon nodded, pride swelling in his chest. They had faced Artemis's evil and emerged victorious. If hope remained, she could not prevail.

CHAPTER TWENTY

The day was exhausting.

Lucas's face shone like a beacon, illuminated with pure light. Dressed in a regal, floor-length, purple linen robe, he spun to find Kyrie standing near him. The divine traveler was releasing energy from her palms to help Poseidon hoist the immense silver sheet into place.

Kyrie voiced a warning. "Can you feel it? This oppressive darkness is overwhelming."

In that instance, reality seemed to slow down as the hulking, three-hundred-pound god lost his grip on the gargantuan silver slab. The reverberations of its fall shook through the area until it neared the ground and Kyrie shot out the power from her palms to suspend it midair. With gentle precision, she propped the gleaming metal against the wall of the unfinished holy building.

Poseidon's bellow echoed in response. "Oh, no!" His lifeblood poured from his wound as he floated twenty feet in the air, his powerful, eight-foot frame limp and at the mercy of Kyrie's magical intervention. Lucas watched in horror as the deity descended toward the earth before Kyrie waved her hands and eased him onto the grass below.

Poseidon lay sprawled across the dirt, his colossal body drained of vitality as a river of red pooled around him.

Lucas rushed over to the injured god of the sea. He knelt beside him, cradled his cut hand, and began to send a deep force from his heart to the injury. Within seconds, the cut healed.

Kyrie, holding an Andara crystal, knelt at Poseidon's head, her hands glowing with a brilliant light that radiated healing energy into his broken form. The light from the green crystal seeped through his skin and mended his wounds, and he opened his eyes to find two angelic healers standing before him.

Lucas spoke of the fall and the deep cut in his hand, and how, with prayer communion, they had worked together to heal it. He warned Poseidon of dizziness but reassured him there would be no lasting harm.

The building of the Temple of Poseidon ceased as Lucas lifted the powerful Shamir and secured it within its lead box, tucking it away within his tunic pocket before declaring they must hunt for the demonic spirit. "Let us gather at home, Poseidon," he said. "We can talk there."

The trio retreated to Cleito's home, where they camped. Lucas and Kyrie sauntered onto the patio of the Koi lagoon. Poseidon stretched his arms wide as he circled around the pool area, rage coating his face like a mask.

The previous day's events made Poseidon angry. "Artemis has spawned a Minotaur," he thundered. "A creature created from my very own invention! Years ago, at King Minos's request, I caused a bull to emerge from the sea, which he promised to sacrifice but hid among a herd of oxen. I then cursed Pasiphaë, Minos's daughter, with an unhealthy obsession for this beast!"

Angelic Kyrie shut her amber eyes, touched her heart, and shook her head. "Yes, our encounter with Artemis and the Minotaur today was her taunting you again. I can feel her darkness nearby. I think she caused the shift in the energy we felt earlier."

Lucas shut his eyes and traveled in his mind to Artemis. "Not only has she produced beasts, but Artemis has also called forward monstrous beings from the depths of the planet."

Face ashen, Poseidon, almost losing his balance, found a chair and sat down. "I cannot believe Artemis would fabricate such wickedness. She has always been jealous of her twin, Apollo. Her ambition could have been to surpass his power. I know what it means to be jealous of a sibling. I often feel irritated with my brother Zeus."

Poseidon gazed out the window at the new island. The hub of Atlantis could be seen in the distance, denoted by three rings of soil and water.

Poseidon's Temple, the major attraction of Cleito's hill's three rings, celebrated the mystical teachings of the Sacred Heart. So high that it disappeared into space, the spire reached through the clouds. They adorned the spire with a magnificent Star of Hope, featuring eight sides and a bridge leading to a small circle below its peak.

Circled by a thin gold ring, the moon connected the Atlanteans to heaven. A wider ring made of silver surrounded the sun, representing its power and glory, while a third star, painted with precious minerals and stones, sat next to it in total luminescence like divine trinity.

Metalwork embraced both earthly technology and spiritual knowledge; beyond this world, Lucas taught them that humans were children of many fathers: biological, scientific, spiritual.

In each direction stood several shrines in perfect circles, ready for completion with a Temple of Healing to be built in warm earth tones near green fields overlooking rolling hills teeming with life; a Temple of Learning dressed in white stone by ocean waters sparkling like diamonds because of the rocky shoreline; a Temple of Records dressed in red sandstone reminiscent of Mars' distant land and, last but not least, a Temple of Leadership, which was raised upon an artificial hill crowned with marble tiles displaying the eight-sided crest of The Way.

Poseidon's Temple would be the Temple of Light and Religious Worship. Perched atop each were two twenty-foot obelisks; like lightning rods, they were ready to draw energy from the stars into the holy palaces.

The oceanic god spoke. "When Atlantis is complete, it will have three provinces with sacred shrines on each ring, demonstrating cosmic harmony between opposites."

Divine light made each step forward possible, coming down from the heavens and creating a bright future for the people of Atlantis.

Poseidon gazed upon the temple, still standing tall despite Artemis's assault. The marble columns, inlaid with lapis lazuli in intricate geometric patterns, gleamed in the sunlight. This sanctuary honoring the sea would withstand anything his bitter niece threw at it.

Turning to his companions, Poseidon said, "You have my deepest gratitude. Without your courage and skill, Artemis may have succeeded."

Kyrie bowed her head respectfully. "It was an honor to serve our greater purpose."

"I'm just glad my Shamir traps worked," Lucas said with a smile. "We make a good team."

"That we do, my friend." Poseidon placed a hand on the architect's shoulder. "When word spreads of how you defended the temple, all of Atlantis will hail you as heroes."

Lucas rubbed his neck, looking embarrassed. "I did what anyone would do."

"It takes great bravery to stand up to a god," said Kyrie. "You deserve acclaim."

Poseidon nodded. "We will dedicate celebrations and songs to this day. But come, you both must be exhausted."

He imagined them inside the quiet temple. Sunbeams slanted through openings in the domed ceiling, illuminating the altar depicting Poseidon holding his trident, rising from the sea in a chariot drawn by hippocampi.

Tension built in Poseidon's muscular body. His brow furrowed with determination. *This is my homeland. Peace through The Way will prevail. No one, especially a member of my family, will bring danger here.* He mentally began to work out how to deal with Artemis and her despicable ways.

Poseidon heard footsteps coming toward them on the patio. Cleito sauntered into the meeting and reported a knock on the front door. When they opened it, Poseidon's team was astonished to find Madeline, an initiate of the Dark Sun, standing before them with tears streaming down her face. Dressed in a blue silk hooded cape and tunic, her chestnut hair cascading down her shoulders, she seemed desperate for their help.

Poseidon stood to greet their guest. "Madeline, I am surprised to see you. What brings you here?"

Kyries and Lucas stood wondering why someone devoted to the Dark Sun would visit them.

She cautiously spoke. "Lord Poseidon, I must warn you of a grave danger. The Goddess Artemis is planning to make a cruel sacrifice at her temple near the beach tomorrow morning at sunrise, and only you can stop it. I used to believe in her dark powers, but now I stand with whatever cause you are fighting for!"

The group suspected being lured into another trap by Madeline's former mistress.

Poseidon's face was tense as he questioned her. Can we trust this isn't an ambush by Hecate?

Madeline stood strong. "Please trust me. I came here willingly and ask you to come with me."

Lucas looked at Poseidon hesitantly. "Explore the temple. Prepare for swift response if violence occurs."

Kyrie's voice revealed her curiosity: "I've always wanted to see an ancient temple."

CHAPTER TWENTY-ONE

As the sun rose, daybreak was between darkness and light. In the twilight, a soft mist covered Artemis's wood. Two doves cooed, announcing the new day. Slithering through the undergrowth, Artemis's pet serpent, Apep, waited for prey. The serpent stalked the bird as it sang its morning song. A strike from Apep, and the sound of the birds singing ended.

"Did you hear that?" Lucas said as he and Poseidon rambled in the wood to call on his sister Artemis.

"No, I hear nothing," Poseidon replied. "Until a few minutes ago, I listened to the doves cooing. Then everything went quiet. Be careful; there could be predators lurking."

As Kyrie, Lucas, and Poseidon moved closer to Artemis's Temple, Poseidon covered his nose with the sleeve of his tunic to block the rank smell of decaying animals that hung in the air. Tiny winged blowflies buzzed around the open back door.

A fifteen-foot-high sculpture of the Hecate, Goddess of the Black Sun, covered in gold, ebony, silver, and black agate stood as the dominate feature of the ceremonial room. A red silk garment covered the legs and hips.

Decorated with reliefs of animals and bees, the uppermost body with many breasts; It adorned her head with a high-pillared headdress. In her right hand was a tall staff with snakes wrapped around it.

Poseidon tiptoed and followed the chanting to enter the sanctuary. The acrid smell of the night's gory rant made his stomach turn. In the room's corner on the cold granite floor stood Artemis, singing praises to an altar with a pentagram. Blood had soaked her knee-length white tunic.

The dark goddess turned to see Poseidon, Lucas, and Kyrie watching.

"Why, Artemis?" Poseidon bellowed over the cacophony. "Atlantis was to be our sanctuary—a realm of peace and prosperity!"

Artemis snarled, silver hair whipping behind her like a pennant. "You are a fool, Uncle! Humans will never change. Atlantis must be mine to rule alone."

With a guttural cry, Artemis picked up her weapon and slashed at Poseidon. He deflected the blow, but its force sent him staggering back. His heart wrenched at the ferocity of her attack. Had the power truly corrupted her so completely?

A deafening boom of power shook the ground as Poseidon and Artemis clashed.

Poseidon's chiseled jaw clenched, his piercing, sea-green eyes alight with rage and pain. After all these years, how could such a betrayal occur?

In his moment of hesitation, Artemis struck again, driving her ruby-tipped Black Sun stave downward. Poseidon raised his trident in time, the impact vibrating through his arms. As he gazed at his niece's face twisted in malice, doubt and anguish tore through him. How could he subdue her without destroying the bond they'd once shared?

Amidst the battle, Lucas's Shamir flared, and Kyrie's magic clashed with the Black Sun's forces. But Poseidon saw only his niece Artemis, once a beloved companion, now a treacherous enemy. His heart ached with the pain of her betrayal.

"It doesn't have to be like this," Poseidon pleaded with a sorrowful tone.

Artemis's lips curled in a malicious sneer, her face twisted with hatred and defiance. "You've gone too far!" Her grip tightened on her slender, Black Sun, ruby-tipped golden rod, radiating a hostile aura of power that only Poseidon could match. "The time has come for you to show your true colors," she hissed, malice dripping from every syllable.

Poseidon roared in rage and charged forward, driven by a deep desire to protect his beloved Atlantis. His trident clashed against Artemis's rod, the reverberations shaking both gods as they fought.

Lucas and Kyrie moved, weaving their hands together in complex patterns before calling upon the light of the Holy Spirit to create a shield around Poseidon. However, it was not enough to protect him from the sheer force of hatred and stronger power of the Black Sun emanating from Artemis.

Pain twisted Poseidon's heart as he grappled with his own niece, trying to comprehend how she could turn her back on everything they had built together. The beautiful realm of Atlantis, built on knowledge and unity, yet threatened by Artemis's selfish ambitions. But even amid his anguish, Poseidon refused to give up; he would do whatever it took to save Atlantis, and all he held dear.

"You cannot win this fight, Uncle!" she roared, her voice echoing with malicious glee. "My Black Sun will make me mistress of Atlantis! I shall reshape it as I see fit!"

Poseidon's grip tightened on his trident, determination coursing through him. He would not allow his niece to plunge their home into darkness. He let out a mighty cry and surged forward, deflecting blows from Artemis's acolytes with vigorous swipes of his weapon.

Meanwhile, Lucas and Kyrie erected a shimmering barrier of supernatural energy around them, keeping the searing blasts of dark lightning at bay. Sparks flew as Poseidon and Artemis fought harder than ever before, their weapons clashing in a blinding display of skill and strength. Only one would prevail.

Kyrie's angelic voice sliced through the air like a razor, as her plea for swift action echoed in desperation. Andara crystals from Pleiades lacked the power.

Poseidon's fists tightened, and rage surged within him at the sight of his beloved niece Artemis consumed with power and madness. He had to stop her before she lost herself and destroyed them all.

With a thunderous roar, Poseidon charged ahead, the sea roaring wherever he passed. Lucas and Kyrie followed behind, their shield transforming into spear like beams of light that hurled forward to repel Artemis's maleficent spells. The clashing of magic and water shook the realm, yet Poseidon would not yield. For his beloved Atlantis, for his own dear niece … he would prevail!

At the edge of the battlefield stood the Lord of Chaos, an ominous figure that seemed to multiply in numbers as its dark tendrils wound around Poseidon's group.

"Your strength is futile against me, sea god," the Lord of Chaos snarled contemptuously from all directions, its icy voice chilling the surrounding air. Poseidon fought on valiantly, his trident slashing away every ghostly apparition sent against him. But they kept coming, each one eroding his energy further.

Artemis surged forward with new vigor as her sinister magic threatened to overwhelm them all. His heart heavy with sorrow, Poseidon lunged forward to meet her attack, remembering days past when he and his beloved niece explored their underwater world together with joyous abandon.

How had their paths diverged so sharply? Despite Poseidon's attempts to steer her away from the darkness, she had chosen the shadows over him.

Poseidon pleaded for a different outcome.

But Artemis only sneered in contempt. "You can't control me with empty words! I will have what is mine!"

His heart sank with her bitter declaration. Had he failed her somehow? Failed to provide the love and understanding she needed?

No. He would not allow himself doubt. No matter how Artemis had stumbled, Poseidon had to stop her. For Atlantis's sake.

Gathering his strength, Poseidon summoned the darkest depths of the sea and unleashed them in a thunderous tidal wave onto her army. The raging torrents engulfed the shadow warriors as he faced off against Artemis again.

"I won't let you pass," Poseidon intoned. His voice was heavy with sorrow, but his resolve was clear. He would bear this burden for his beloved Atlantis.

Poseidon's arms trembled as he held his trident aloft. The fate of Atlantis depended on this last strike.

Her voice cracked, a raw mix of sadness and defiance. "I tried so hard to prove myself. I was not your equal."

The agony in his chest burned hotter than any physical wound as Poseidon remembered days long gone when she had been nothing more than a little girl pleading with him to play ceaseless games and pursue sea creatures. Now, here she was, face contorted with wrath and an insatiable craving for revenge.

"Why?" Poseidon spat through gritted teeth, blood streaming from a cut above his eye. He had to comprehend why this once loving niece now sought to annihilate him.

She hesitated, bosom heaving under her labored breaths. "You all ignored me," she whispered venomously.

"Father, Hera, even you, ignored my achievements and reduced me to just a woman. Not deserving of genuine power."

"You can recollect me as a playmate in your water realm. But you did not witness me as an adult. I had hoped you would have surpassed the social prejudices against female gods in our culture. Even among the Greek gods, goddesses are inferior to the male gods".

"Didn't it occur to you I could be like you? I once adored you so much. But now … I cannot. I detest you."

The veracity of her words slammed into Poseidon's heart like a bolt of electricity. He understood his pride had clouded his vision and prevented him from seeing Artemis's value.

His heart clenched with regret. Had they all been so blind? He'd begun, "Artemis …"

But she cut him off, ruby lightning slashing through the air. "No more words. Today I take my rightful place."

The niece he had known was gone, replaced by a creature of icy determination whose gaze reached far beyond his own. Poseidon unleashed the ocean's full force, overpowering Artemis's attempt to resist. The crushing blow slammed into her, sweeping her away in a sea of foam and fury.

It was over—or so he thought. When Poseidon approached, each step in an effort, there came a flicker of movement beneath the coral pillar.

Her eyelids fluttered open and fixed him with a piercing stare. "Why didn't you finish it?"

He grasped the pillar, veins bulging as he rippled with an effort to lift it away. Artemis stumbled back in shock, her face a mask of disbelief.

"How can you show me mercy?" she stammered.

"I have no choice."

She trembled, unable to look him in the eye.

"Atlantis will survive," Poseidon said. "And that matters now."

Artemis shivered, hatred lingering in her gaze. But Poseidon caught a glimmer of his niece beneath all the pain and sorrow. Perhaps she could find redemption one day.

Then he strode forward with a thundering voice, trident blazing like a beacon of light that shone forth a path of hope.

CHAPTER TWENTY-TWO

Poseidon turned to Lucas, Kyrie, and Cleito. "Let us return home and develop our next move with Artemis. Her darkness may not stay here on Atlantis."

With a deadened heart, Poseidon went sadly back to the house. He had no alternative but to take severe measures.

They sat in the dining room, unsure of their next move.

Lucas relaxed back in his chair. With his heart, he connected with each person. He adopted a tone rich with understanding and acceptance. His love touched each person. "I know it was hard to be there with Artemis and watch her turn away from our help. I am glad we tried. Life lessons on handling change involve the heart and mind. People change for two reasons: They open their attitudes to a new direction, or their broken hearts are ready to heal."

Cleito desired to comprehend Lucas's thoughts on life lessons. What life lessons help navigate the mind through change?

"I am glad you asked," Lucas said. "Artemis closed off her heart because of the resentment of being dismissed as a woman.

It made her angry when she tried to be creative, only to be dismissed. Insisting on having her way, she will use her mind and personal power to be in control."

The Teacher investigated Artemis's heart. "More lessons await her, making life difficult. The energy of light has opposites, like the sun and moon, light and darkness. There is always a choice about the path one responds to change."

"One key to moving through life's challenges is forgiveness. It takes courage from the spiritual heart to face the pain and begin the journey to sense you are whole." The Teacher paused. Loving energy filled the room, holding a peaceful serenity. "We can use the inner light energy in the spiritual heart in various ways."

"Artemis seems lost because she has cut off her heart and lives in darkness. It's time to leave her alone. We can let her know we support her. When she is ready to come home to her loving family, we will be here to assist her in her journey back to her spiritual heart."

Poseidon had to make a hard decision. He sat up straight in his chair with a voice of authority. "The peace of The Way is being interrupted. We must remove Artemis before she does more harm. Her abilities as a human hybrid and goddess surpass those of a mortal and could cause a lot of destruction. I do not want her to disrupt our peace. I propose we remove her."

"Using my trident with the Shamir Stone and you, Lucas, with the sacred light, we can carve out her place of darkness and its territory and set it on the unnamed isle we made. She can have her evil practices there. Hopefully, she'll move past her sorrow and come back to us. Does anyone have a better solution?"

Kyrie, Lucas, and Cleito shook their heads.

CHAPTER TWENTY-THREE

Artemis heard a knock on the window where she sat. In the moonlight, she saw a boy with a letter. The goddess walked over to the open window, where the messenger handed her a folded parchment marked with a red seal of Atlantis. She took the missive and opened it. Holding the paper, she read:

> My dearest sister, Artemis, I am sorry you are so unhappy. It is with great sadness your living on Atlantis and practicing your dark magic is unacceptable.
>
> Since you are determined to take a dark path, I have planned to remove you, your wicked chamber, and anyone who follows you to a landmass far from Atlantis. To do this, Lucas and I will cut out your structure and surrounding acreage at sunrise tomorrow morning from the earth of Atlantis. Then we

will transport it to an unnamed atoll that Lucas and I created. Perhaps you will find peace there. My aim is to safeguard my family, The Way, and Atlantis's people's peaceful and prosperous living. Cleito and I are available to support you in releasing your dark practices.

We can help you in living a happier life if you choose. Until then, goodbye, dear niece.

Your loving uncle, Poseidon.

Artemis sat, stunned. She jumped up and down with excitement. *Move me? How perfect.* The idea of having her own place energized her.

The dawn of early morning broke with an earthquake. Artemis woke with the thunder of moving earth. She ran to one column at the halfway point of her sanctuary and hung on for dear life. The shifting building and earth beneath tumbled furniture, glassware, statues—everything was in shambles. Then she transformed herself into a hawk and fled.

Poseidon stood with his golden trident. He swept the sky with a bolt of lightning. His staff charged with electrical current.

With the Shamir's laser, Lucas dug into the earth using his staff.

Lucas stood next to Poseidon, chanting sacred tones of light and energy. The two moved together like a dance. Energy of light and sound from Lucas energized Shamir to cut deep into the earth.

Poseidon, God of Earthquakes, removed from the surrounding area the earth cutting as Lucas aided in positioning the new earth.

Poseidon, with his human hybrid strength, boosted the reliquary.

The Andara crystals attached to the parapet tore like missiles in all directions. With his heart and mind, Lucas moved the monument with the parcel they established when they created Cleito Hill. The entire operation took less than thirty minutes.

With Artemis settled in her new home, Poseidon felt satisfied he had done everything he could to help his niece and save his people. The terrain's deep gash transformed the shrine's spot into a small pond. Water from deep within the Atlantean water aquifer began to fill the hole. Water blessed and cleansed the darkness, which was now gone.

The shattered remains of the once grand temple lay strewn across the charred earth. Pillars of blackened marble jutted at odd angles amid piles of rubble. The air was heavy with the acrid smell of smoke and ash.

Poseidon surveyed the devastation, his eyes narrowing as they traced over the scorch marks marring the ground. The sea god's fists clenched, knuckles white. This had been no ordinary fire.

Beside him stood Lucas, a slender frame draped in a gossamer robe that shimmered as he moved. The mystical traveler's ageless face creased with concern as he placed a comforting hand on Poseidon's shoulder.

"Her darkness runs deep," Lucas said, his voice resonant yet gentle. "But it is not the end. The light is bright in Atlantis."

Poseidon's jaw tightened, bitterness welling up inside him. "My brother Zeus claims to rule with wisdom and justice. Yet he allowed his daughter to do this. He spoke with clipped words and simmering anger in his voice."

Gazing upon the Traveler's tranquil features, Poseidon felt the tempest within him quiet. It was true what Lucas said—judging

Zeus was not a simple matter. One could not restore their loss by dwelling on the past.

Poseidon turned his focus to the space where the dark temple had once stood. They had damaged the dark temple on the outer structure, but its foundations were still intact, so Poseidon turned his focus toward it.

"We will continue to build," he declared.

Closing his eyes, Poseidon spread his arms wide. He envisioned the rubble clearing, the scorched ground transforming. Lucas added his energies to the work, their combined power rippling outward.

The earth rumbled, shifting, and settling. Stones drew together, fused, and smoothed. From deep below, clear water began bubbling up, filling the contours of the land. Within moments, a round pond shone beneath the sun, its surface smooth as glass.

Poseidon opened his eyes, beholding their creation. They'd banished the darkness. Hope glimmered anew.

Poseidon gazed upon the shimmering pond, this symbol of Atlantis's renewal. Though Artemis's darkness had marred the land, it would not prevail. Poseidon focused his energies, calling upon the powers of the sea.

Waves crashed in the distance as he summoned their force. The waters responded to his command, rushing forth and filling the pond. The level rose, fed by the god's divine will.

Lucas added his strengths, manipulating strands of light into being. They danced across the surface, illuminating the pond with their glow. Together, their cosmic abilities transformed space. Radiant waters replaced shadows.

Poseidon waded in up to his knees, his chiton billowing. With arms outstretched, he guided the currents, envisioning the grand temple restored. Lucas stood atop the water, strands of light swirling around him. His very presence purified any lingering darkness.

As the pond took shape, abalone shells edged the border, their pearly hues glinting. Poseidon smiled, knowing this haven would welcome all seekers. Though the path remained difficult, this cleansing brought hope. The light would rise again.

Poseidon's expression turned solemn as he surveyed the pond. "Much work remains. Artemis's darkness runs deep."

Lucas nodded, his ageless eyes filled with wisdom. "Yet this light will guide the way. Have faith, my friend."

Poseidon sighed, the weight of his burdens clear. "I fear faith alone is not enough. Action must follow intent."

"As it will," Lucas reassured. "But beginnings arise from inner realms. What manifests without first emerges from within."

Poseidon contemplated his words. Perhaps renewal relied not on grand gestures but subtle stirrings of the soul. If hearts turned toward light, darkness would fade.

"Come," Lucas said. "Let us walk."

They strolled along the pond's edge in contemplative silence. The soft lapping of the water soothed Poseidon's spirit. Overhead, gulls cried, welcoming the new dawn.

Poseidon turned toward Lucas. "Your counsel lifts my spirits, ancient one. The path seems less obscured."

Lucas smiled. "The way is in flow, not force. Be the calm current, steadfast yet serene."

Comforted, Poseidon gazed outward. The first rays of sun broke over the distant sea. Atlantis would rise, its foundations rebuilt—not through struggle, but surrender. By yielding to higher forces, the light would prevail.

Poseidon and Lucas continued their stroll along the serene pond, appreciating the tranquility that now filled the space where Artemis's darkness once festered.

Poseidon paused, bending down to trail his fingers through the clear water. Ripples spread outward in concentric circles, catching the rays of the morning sun. He smiled softly, taking in the simple beauty. "It seems almost unbelievable," he murmured. "Emergence of light from shadows."

Lucas nodded. "Yet the deepest darkness often births the brightest dawn. Twisted roots, when torn away, create fertile soil for fresh growth."

Poseidon considered this, comforted by the thought. Even Artemis's malevolence could not stop Atlantis's rebirth.

As they walked on, a flock of white birds took flight from a nearby tree. Poseidon tracked their graceful ascent, his spirits lifting with their upturned wings.

"Behold the signs," Lucas said, following his gaze. "Life returns, undeterred by the darkness of yesterday."

The breeze picked up, carrying the smell of blooming wildflowers. Poseidon breathed deeply, filling his lungs with the sweet air. The land itself seemed cleansed, revitalized.

"Come, let us sit awhile." Lucas gestured toward a stone bench overlooking the pond. Poseidon joined him, both gazing out at the shimmering waters. A sense of peace filled the air.

"The past fades," Lucas whispered. "New light dawns. Have confidence in yourself. Your strength will steer Atlantis through the coming tides."

Reassured, Poseidon let his doubts drift away in the morning breeze. As predicted by Lucas, the darkness was now behind them. Ahead lay only light and hope.

Poseidon nodded, comforted by Lucas's wisdom. This Mystic Traveler had a way of illuminating the truth, helping Poseidon see beyond his own limitations.

They sat in contemplative silence for some time, watching the play of light across the pond's surface. Footsteps sounded on the path behind them.

Poseidon turned to see Cleito's eyes widening as she took in the land's transformation. "It's beautiful," she said, joining Lucas and Poseidon on the bench. "I can't believe this was once her shrine."

Lucas smiled knowingly. "The past fades; the new light dawns. Have faith in this process."

Cleito met Poseidon's eyes, understanding passing between them. After all they had weathered, hope emerged triumphant.

New life was burgeoning, and darkness banished. Poseidon acknowledged Lucas's words. Though trials still lay ahead, he would face them with faith in himself and in fate's unfolding design.

Poseidon gazed out over the shimmering pond, taking in the scene's tranquility. We have replaced the shadows and pain of this place with light and promise.

"A fitting transformation," he remarked. "I have cleansed the darkness from this site."

Lucas nodded. "Yes, the cleansing was much needed. This act will have far-reaching effects.

Poseidon's eyes followed the ripples moving across the pond. "It is a new beginning for Atlantis," he said. "With Artemis gone, we build something better."

Lucas agreed it was time for renewal. "You must lead your people toward the light, Poseidon."

Poseidon considered this duty. For too long, bitterness and anger had clouded his vision. But the fog was lifting; he saw now where his focus must lie.

"I will lead them," he vowed, his voice ringing with conviction. "We will forge a new Atlantis, guided by hope instead of fear."

Lucas clasped his shoulder. "You have found your purpose, my friend. Go forth and let it shine."

A sense of peace filled Poseidon, along with renewed strength and clarity. The future awaited bright with promise. He would meet it with wisdom, compassion, and unwavering dedication to Atlantis.

The pond was a symbol of the triumph over darkness, and the victory of light. Gazing at its calm surface, Poseidon felt only hope for what was to come.

CHAPTER TWENTY-FOUR

Five Years Later

Poseidon emerged from the swirling sea, dark hair flowing behind him as he strode onto the shores of Atlantis. His piercing eyes, filled with brooding intensity, scanned the landscape before him. This was his kingdom, risen from the depths by his own hand. Now, returning from his odyssey beyond the mortal realm, he wore a new mantle of purpose.

No longer consumed by bitterness toward Zeus, Poseidon's heart held a nascent hope. Though his imposing presence still commanded awe and respect from those around him, a deeper wisdom now tempered his moods like the ever-shifting tides.

As he walked, the sand seemed to solidify beneath his feet, acknowledging its creator. Beside him came Cleito, her very presence illuminating the way forward. Though her lineage contained echoes of Poseidon's ancient past, she now stood as his equal.

Her eyes, brimming with compassion, told of revelations from their journey. Yet beneath her warmth, she too nursed the scars of her beginnings. Together with Euenor, Lucas, Leucippus, and Kyrie, they had forged bonds of fellowship. But uncertainty still loomed over Atlantis's horizon.

Poseidon turned to Cleito. "We are home, returned to the shores I raised from the deep. Atlantis needs more work to become a beacon of hope and harmony between worlds." His voice boomed like crashing waves, yet his words carried the weight of newfound humility.

Cleito nodded, linking her arm through his. "The path ahead is long," she replied. "But we no longer walk it alone."

Cleito's radiant beauty shone like a beacon as she walked beside Poseidon along the shimmering shores of Atlantis. Her long, flowing hair cascaded down her back in waves, glinting golden in the sunlight like the glimmering sea. Yet her smiling eyes now held a wisdom that spoke of growth beyond her years. A light kindled from their transformative journey.

Where once she had seemed but a youthful innocent, now Cleito carried herself with a grace that bespoke inner strength and insight. Gazing out across the waters that had birthed the realm, she measured her steps in an unhurried manner.

Beside her strode Euenor, his graying hair and beard lending him an air of calm authority. The lines on his weathered face told of knowledge hard won, his steady eyes speaking of revelations gathered over long years of searching. He walked with the confidence of one who has glimpsed truths beyond most mortals' ken.

Yet for all his wisdom, Euenor's gaze held a glint of joyful relief at returning to familiar shores. Atlantis meant more than just a homeland to him; it symbolized hope for a harmonious future.

As the small group passed, the people of Atlantis paused in their daily tasks to bow their heads in deference. But their eyes shone with gladness at the safe return of Poseidon and Cleito, the father and mother who linked gods and humans in kinship.

Poseidon met the eyes of his people, accepting their wordless welcome with a solemn nod. For the first time since leaving the ocean's depths, the weight of responsibility settled upon his shoulders once more. The bitterness was no longer present in him. In its place, a newfound sense of purpose kindled on his journey alongside Cleito's and the others'.

Turning to Euenor, Poseidon clasped the older man's shoulder. "Much building lies ahead, my friend. But we will do it together."

Lucas drifted along the path, his slender frame seeming to float above the earth. An ethereal glow emanated from his pale skin, casting dancing shadows on the rocks and trees around him. His eyes were pools of liquid silver that reflected no light, only infinite depth. They gazed ahead, seeing far beyond the material plane surrounding him.

Though he spoke little, his very presence brought comfort and guidance to those around him. Poseidon found himself drawn to the mystic, sensing hidden wells of ancient wisdom within. Cleito watched Lucas with curiosity, wondering what insights he could share about her own clouded past.

Only Leucippus kept her distance, averting her eyes whenever Lucas looked her way. She seemed diminished; her delicate beauty had faded since their journey began. The nymph's thoughts turned inward, preoccupied with memories and secrets long suppressed.

Cleito felt a pang in her heart as she looked into Leucippus's haunted eyes. Whatever her mother's past transgressions, Cleito knew Leucippus had acted out of misguided love. Taking her hand, Cleito whispered reassurances only the two of them could hear.

At her touch, the tension in Leucippus's body eased. Mother and daughter continued together, the gulf between them not yet bridged, but no longer insurmountable. Ahead lay tough truths to be faced. But united by blood and shared hardship, they would confront the past with open hearts.

The ragged cliffs of Atlantis rose before them, sea spray mingling with their tears.

Poseidon's piercing gaze took in the distant spires and towers of the Atlantean kingdom rising from the shimmering sea. For a moment, bitterness stirred in his heart. This was not Olympus, the realm denied him by his brother Zeus. But the feeling soon passed. Atlantis was his to shape, free from the petty grievances of the gods.

As they drew nearer, signs of life emerged along the rocky coast. Fishermen with bronzed skin and lean muscles called out greetings. Children with wild hair and sea-bright eyes stopped their play to stare. Women in flowing dresses whispered and pointed as the strange company passed by.

At the head of the procession strode Kyrie, her steps light despite the long journey. Otherworldly grace marked her every movement, hinting at her Pleiadean origins. She walked neither with the group nor apart from it, a reminder that her purpose was higher than any faction's.

Euenor strolled side by side with Poseidon, his brilliant blue eyes sweeping across the city they had created. A spark of pride flashed across his seasoned face, yet reverence kept it from flaring too high. The genuine work was just beginning—establishing harmony between all beings and realms.

Even Lucas found himself mesmerized by the panoramic sight of Atlantis. His sharp intuition penetrated deeper than most, and he could feel a potent energy stirring beneath its breathtaking beauty. Lucas's sage like wisdom shed light on each person's individual purpose.

Poseidon felt hope begin to swell within him, nurtured by trials he and Euenor had endured together. Away from Zeus's domain, he was determined to build something that would last beyond these petty feuds among gods. With Cleito—his love—at his side, Poseidon hoped to establish a utopia of knowledge, rather than an empire of violence.

A sense of mission filled Poseidon's heart as the majestic Kingdom of Atlantis stretched before him, energetically calling out for The Way.

Poseidon's piercing gaze swept over the bustling streets of Atlantis, taking in the fruits of his labors. Vibrant hues of crimson, azure, and gold adorned the splendid buildings that lined the thoroughfares.

Merchants called out their wares, while children laughed and played games of chase. The very air hummed with industry and joyful chatter. He spotted Madeline with her friends, walking carefree in the summer breeze.

This was the realm he had carved from the sea for his beloved Cleito. A haven of prosperity, knowledge, and beauty. The journey had only strengthened his resolve to cultivate Atlantis into a shining beacon among humanity's scattered lights.

Poseidon strode onward through the parting crowds, his companions arrayed around him in unity. The diverse talents and insights they embodied would help steer Atlantis toward its lofty purpose.

No room for gods' pettiness here. Poseidon turned his back on those toxic patterns. With Cleito's wisdom, Euenor's counsel,

Lucas's foresight, and Kyrie's mediation, Atlantis might become a realm of enlightenment and amity. A worthy legacy for ages to come.

Much remained uncertain, but Poseidon squared his shoulders against the challenges ahead. He would steer fate's currents as masterfully as he commanded the seas. None would redefine Atlantis's destiny but him.

The sun glinted off distant spires, hinting at hidden potential. Poseidon's eyes gleamed with purpose. The genuine work had just begun.

Cleito walked alongside Poseidon, her gentle smile radiating warmth. She placed a hand on his arm, drawing his gaze. "My love," she whispered. "Words cannot express my gratitude for the bond we now share. My heart holds the most valuable understanding from this journey."

Poseidon covered her hand with his own. "It is I who should thank you. Your wisdom and compassion will be Atlantis's guiding light."

Cleito shook her head. "You give me too much credit. We shall walk this path together."

Poseidon pulled her close. The challenges ahead seemed less daunting, with Cleito at his side. Her presence was a balm to his spirit, just as the sea soothed him.

Euenor approached and clasped Poseidon's shoulder. "Well done, my friend. Your achievements make me very proud."

Poseidon met the older man's approving gaze. "I owe much to your guidance, Euenor. Your counsel will steer us through uncertain waters."

"As long as we hold to our purpose, the way will become clear," Euenor replied. "Differences fade before humanity's common threads."

Kyrie drifted over, her movements graceful and ethereal. With graceful and ethereal movements, Kyrie planted the seeds of understanding. With patience and dedication, they will blossom.

Lucas materialized in a shimmer of light. "The future remains unshaped. But we now possess the wisdom to mold it toward harmony."

Leucippus hovered nearby, a small smile playing on her lips. They had banished the shadows of her past. A new day dawned on them all.

United in vision and purpose, Poseidon and his companions turned toward the heart of Atlantis. An air of optimism filled their hearts. The trials ahead paled beside the radiance of their bond. Together, they shape the future.

EPILOGUE

THE RED FALCON SPREAD HER WINGS FROM THE WOODLAND high in the mountains of Atlantis to her shattered refuge on Aryan Island. Artemis, the goddess of the wood, seemed regal, flying above. When transformed into a human, she looked disheveled. Still clothed in a dried, blood-soaked tunic, her hair matted with her bare feet, she stood in the sand near her new involuntary home.

The deity, with her right hand over her brow, surveyed the flat dirt landmass. She saw her demolished shrine. Like a twister, her place of safety flew from Atlantis and crashed on the shore of Aryan Island. She chose the name Aryan because she would create a pure race of people. With the priest-scientist she had recruited from Atlantis and their knowledge of DNA manipulation, the new, pure-breed race would be Aryan. She would sacrifice anyone whose blood they believed was impure.

Feeling overwrought and self-conscious, not sure of what to do next, her highness dropped into the dirt. She scraped her hair and tucked it behind her ear. Blinking rapidly, her face flushed, she began a strangled laugh.

Jumping up, the goddess devised a new plan. Her head tilted to the side, cheeks flushed pink, chest puffed out as Artemis began to clap her hands together. She called her father's name, beckoning him to come now.

Through a haze of smoke, the king of the gods appeared. His arms crossed, he leaned away from his daughter, his mind distracted. "What do you want? I was having a spicy moment with Aphrodite."

For a few seconds, Zeus studied Artemis. "What have you been doing? You look a mess and smell like you have been rolling in something nasty." Looking around, he asked, "What is this place? Where are we?"

Flinching, Artemis forgot her state of dress and began to move back from her father. She threw back her tangled hair, dropped her eyes. "Sorry, no time for freshening up. I must see you," Artemis said, motioning to a broken step in her sanctuary for them to sit. She began to feel sorry for herself and told her father what happened on Atlantis with Poseidon.

Zeus groaned in outrage and disbelief. He shook his lengthy salt-and-pepper locks in despair. "My brother tore you and your shrine from Atlantis, then tossed you, without regard, here?" He examined the dumped stone monument on the flat dirt landmass. "What do you want me to do? Do you want to stay here?"

Daddy's girl lifted her puffy azure eyes, blinked her eyelashes. "Poseidon has Atlantis and his movement, The Way. He thought what I was doing would interfere with his precious peace. I want to create Aryan Island, where I can get my revenge on him. What I want is an army like the Spartans, who will help crush him. Then I will take his Atlantis and build more of an empire for you."

"You want me to help you create an army? You will need a fortress. Look around here. This is a deserted island." Zeus barked a laugh. "You have got to be joking."

"Please, Father, I need you to convince my brother Ares, the God of War, to help me."

"Your brother is a loose cannon. He is brutal. Did you see the disaster he invented in Troy?"

"Yes, but that is what I need. He is a savage. Ares is perfect. Can you talk to him about me? He knows how to build a fortress. Tell him I will sacrifice a bull for him. He realizes how Poseidon reveres his creation of the bull. If I surrender one of Poseidon's sacred animals, he will do anything I ask. His blood lust is endless."

Zeus's face showed concern and deep thought with a smile. He bent back his head and stroked his beard. He had to manage his brother and the new empire, Atlantis. Artemis's idea of a military fortress and DNA lab may work. "All right; I will talk to Ares. His reputation needs repair after his last battle in Troy. He sided with the defeated Trojans against the Greeks with Athena's aid. He has been sulking ever since." Zeus looked at his daughter with a knowing smile. "Whatever you do, make sure your new isle is something my brother envies."

Artemis replied. "But Daddy, don't tell him what I am doing. I want to surprise him."

Zeus nodded his head. "Poseidon won't hear a word from me. I promise." With a snap of his fingers, Zeus disappeared.

The demigod began her happy dance. Her feet, in a wide stance, fists on her hips, threw her matted hair up into the air as she screamed, "Poseidon, I am coming for you." She pranced, humming, into the water to bathe.

A forest creature, Artemis loathed to wash. She enjoyed rolling in the leaves and muck with her jungle friends. The smell of the animal world was how creatures stalked their prey. The female scent when in heat was important for the copulating season. A too-clean, fresh goddess who ruled them was hard to convince the creatures of the woodland she was their leader. She needed to impress Ares, who loved a feisty woman's scent.

Splashing in the warm sea, Artemis dove to the sandy bottom and found a sponge with which to wash herself. She pulled the brownish, round swab from its nesting and began to scrub the crusty dirt from her frame. While she floated on the water, the goddess called the minnows to clean her hair.

When her body was refreshed, she walked onto the shore. With her mind, she designed a knee-length, blue-green tunic tied with a gold sash, which wrapped around her shape like a flawless glove. She looked down at her bare feet. Should she put on sandals? *No, why do I need to cover my feet?* Bright and clean, Artemis was ready to greet her brother Ares.

When the god of war arrived on the islet, he was immediately unimpressed with the bleak lack of vegetation and resources. The goddess's monument leaned into the dirt with limestone columns scattered in pieces over the ground. Fully clad in his gleaming Greek, bronze warrior armor helmet and treasured golden fleece over his knee-length black tunic, he turned to Artemis.

"What? Father said you asked for my help, but your barren island needs a rebuild from the ground up. How do you see this desolate place in the future?"

The goddess of the wood greeted her brother. "Well, hello to you, too. Yes, I know the place needs work. I wanted to review what goes where and how. The good news is we have a clean slate. I know one of your gifts is that you can shapeshift anything. So where do we begin?"

Artemis told her brother of her idea of building a fortress on Aryan. With scientists recruited from Atlantis, she would use DNA to create a race of pure human hybrids.

With a workforce of her making, she would create a business for the world of changing animals into giants using DNA. She did not tell him of her vision to destroy Poseidon on Atlantis. Ares was close to his Uncle Poseidon.

The god of war's eyes lit up with delight. "Wow, what a great idea, to use DNA to make human hybrids! Maybe you could help me develop a new army of super soldiers. That would be cool." The fiery leader shaped the new world with his ambition.

Aryan began as a configuration of wild and rugged interior covered in dense forests and steep cliffs. A variety of wild animals, including deer, bears, and wolves, began to run free in their new home with Artemis as their protector.

Ares used his gift of teleportation to move several small villages of humans, who lived off the countryside, from Greece to their new homeland.

With the stone of Artemis's demolished monument, Ares used his knowledge of warfare and military strategy to design the fortress, while Artemis contributed her knowledge of the terrain and the animals that lived on it. They worked together tirelessly, using their divine powers to move massive stones and shape the terrain to their will. Aryan people watched in awe and gratitude as the fortress took shape. Artemis and Ares provided protection from all threats.

The fortress was a stunning success of engineering and design, a testament to the power of Artemis and Ares working together. An impenetrable stronghold. The fortress, built with divine help, would protect Aryan for years.

When the fortress was complete, Ares said, "I can't wait to show Uncle Poseidon what we have designed. He will be so proud of me."

Artemis sucked in a breath. *Poseidon can't know about our plans.* "No, no, no, Ares. We must create an army to go with our fortress. We need a few Spartans to make into hybrid superhuman soldiers."

Removing his golden helmet, Ares wiped the sweat from his brow. "We can improve our army to surpass Athena's puny Greek army in Troy. I am leaving now to handpick one hundred volunteer Spartans."

Artemis held out her hand to her brother for a handshake. "I will find the scientists for the DNA work and contact you when Operation Human Hybrid Soldier is ready to begin."

The demigod of darkness, Hecate, former goddess of the wood, Artemis, looked on with approval and felt secure in her new homeland.

Evening stars began to appear as the light turned into darkness. While satisfied with her creation, she still felt a need in her heart.

www.ingramcontent.com/pod-product-compliance
Lightning Source LLC
Chambersburg PA
CBHW020657120726
47906CB00001B/314